Days of Our Zombies

Tom and Kelly were always meant to be together, until he left for the police academy, and something occurred. Something so big, that she broke off their budding relationship without any explanation.

Kelly has a secret. One so big and destructive that it changed the whole path of her life and made it impossible to be with Tom, the one man she's always loved. And still does.

Tom is learning a lot about the things that changed his life. About his father, and Kelly. What he now knows would have destroyed him in the past, but now he knows the truth, he's desperate to find a way to breach the distance between them. Except zombies aren't going to give them the time Tom needs to fix the shattered trust between them.

When they learn about the zombie evolution, and how much more dangerous they've become to their island community. He's working right alongside her, and trying to show Kelly that she can both trust him, and his love.

All they have to do is survive.

The Zombiology World... So far

The Reset

A zombie apocalypse is here, but figuring out how to survive in the immediate aftermath is only the first step.

Elaine is just an ordinary woman, but when the apocalypse occurs, she must find a way to survive in an increasingly hostile world. Enter Liam, the policeman who saves her at their first meeting and provides assistance as they try to cope with the zombie outbreak brought about by an unknown infection that's spreading out of control.

Together they form a community, trying to save as many lives as they can, a place where people can be safe. Even in the throes of disaster though, emotions creep up, taking both of them by surprise. Who knows? They might just get their happy ever after...if they can survive.

I Dream of Zombies

After the apocalypse the world was a different place. Those who survived did so by wits, strength and by banding together.

Julia is a soldier—not by choice but circumstance in a world where taking up arms is a necessity. She's buried the softer parts of herself including her heart.

Leroy on the other hand is a warrior. An ex-soldier who has to come to terms with what he hides and a loner by choice.

Now they have a mission—retrieve those missing from *Camp Queanbeyan*. Survival is just the first step on a rocky road toward redemption and there's no guarantee of success.

Six Million Dollar Zombie

What do you get in the middle of a zombie apocalypse when you mix Canberra, a Priest and Kindergarten teacher?

Sparks. Lots of red-hot sparks of passion.

Dove may be a priest, but he's also a man and he's been alone for a long time. Rescuing Leonie by the side of the road is just the first step on a journey no one expected to love.

Leonie is running. Her family is gone, the zombies are chasing her, and she's rescued by a priest on a motorbike and taken to a community which welcomes her.

Life should only get better, but the forces who began the apocalypse are building an army of mutated, super-strong zombies. They plan to overtake everything those in the communities have built.

Times are only going to get tougher until they can defeat those with no interest in survival.

Make Room For Zombies

The Zombie Invasion—a failed government experiment—continues to spread...

When Adrienne makes the decision to pack up her infant twins, Leanne and Fiona, and make for an island, she has no idea just how much her life will change. The young widowed mother of two-month-old twins can't stay where she's been, because they're demanding more than she can give. They need her to be a warrior—something she isn't. The only option is to run to the idyllic island off the coast of Queensland.

The island might be cut off from the mainland with just one fortified bridge, but Jack knows it won't take much for the zombies to invade. With a half baked plan to blow up the bridge and the self-proclaimed mayor missing in action, he doesn't really need more responsibility.

That is until he meets Addie and the babies. Now, he's got so much more at stake than just the islanders protection. He's got a ready made family, if they can just survive the next few weeks.

Only time will tell, especially when zombies are involved.

THE ZOMBIOLOGY NOVELS

Zombies in Australia...

and there's more to come!

DAYS OF OUR ZOMBIES

A Zombieology Novel

Imogene Nix

Please note:

The UK and USA share the English language, but there are many words that are spelled differently. Some words have extra letters in the British spelling, such as the word cancelled. In American English, it is spelled canceled. There also words that interchange the letters c or s and sometimes z. For example, in America, you spell offense and in Britain, it is written as offence. We also use the letter u in many words, such as colour and flavour. These spellings are **not** incorrect.

We also have alternative words. Nappy, for example, is used in place of diaper and these are not incorrect terms, simply those appropriate in an Australian setting.

Also, please note:

Local Government is the term used in Australia to describe a City Council or Municipal Authority and is considered the third tier of government.

This book is written in UK English to reflect my Australian/English background.

PROLOGUE

Kelly looked out at the water, the same body of sea that had always soothed her ragged nerves. Nothing was the same. Nothing could ever be the same.

"Dad, I wish you hadn't left me." Tears burned, and nothing took away the pain that radiated deep inside her chest. The sense of aloneness was more than she could bear. Her future here on the island was now a question she couldn't find an easy answer for. So much had changed in only a couple of years.

Sand whirled in eddies around her feet.

Once, she'd have thought she'd have someone to face this with. She'd been so sure in her teen years…well, at least until that fateful day. Now her future was a desolate wasteland.

It would be so easy…

The refrain she'd battled with for years, the one she'd been so sure she'd beaten back until her father's death, gnawed at her. Her wrist itched, and she rubbed it absently. Just as she always did.

"I will not let you win." She turned and left the sandy shore, her feet making hushed whoofing noises as she made her way to the grassy edges and toward the cabin where she'd lived most of her life.

She had tasks to accomplish, a game face to put on, and a life to live.

***

Thomas looked again at the crumpled page on his desk. The same one he'd been looking at for months. He knew the words intimately, having read them so many times. 'Case closed' and 'lack of evidence' had jumped out at him. It was bad enough his mother had never let on, nor had his father. They'd kept the truth from him, the same way everyone around him who may have known did, and when he returned from the academy, there'd been not a word. Even worse, he couldn't be sure they hadn't kept quiet because his father had threatened those around him.

The day Kelly had handed the missive to him, on the jetty, he'd been so sure, but doubts rose, and he'd decided to look through his parents' things. The stuff he'd simply shoved into cartons when they'd passed. And the truth was there in black and white. The diaries his father had religiously kept but hidden until after he'd served his time in prison for fraudulently appropriating the retirement savings of his clients.

The way he'd crowed when he'd returned and the sad look in his mother's eyes. It was all a kind of truth he'd avoided, even though he'd seen the signs. After he'd been trained to discern truths... His father's comments every time he and Kelly had gone out. The crass comments about 'getting some jiggy time.'

The diary in his hands though, that was damning.

The stupid bitch. I asked her to tell her parents to not press charges. Or at the least to have Tom testify. The whole time she stood there, looking at me like I was some kind of worm. Teasing me with nipples erect under the swimsuit. What was a man supposed to do? Ignore the come-on? The fucking nuns got in the way. I only got a taste of the girl, not even a decent grope. If I get my hands on her again, I'll teach her a lesson she won't soon forget.

The contents of Thomas' gut curdled. He'd let Kelly down on the jetty, the same way he'd let her down all those years ago, even though he'd been too young and immature to understand it.

"Fuck." He dropped his now aching head into shaking hands. Facing these truths was nothing short of horrifying.

A knocking came from his office door and his best friend, Jack, entered the room. "What's wrong?"

Thomas squeezed his eyes shut for a second, then looked up. "I've been a fool. A blind fucking tool of a fool at that."

Jack's face creased. "I doubt that's the case, but I needed to let you know that Kelly's dad died. They've taken his remains to the crematorium."

He almost reeled. "Kelly's dad?" He sounded like a fucking parrot, but the words refused to lodge in his brain.

"Yeah. Addie was going to stay with her, but she wanted time alone. I thought..."

Thomas knew exactly what jack was thinking. Only, he didn't have the right to intrude now. Probably never would again. The invisible knife thrust deeper into his aching chest.

"I..." Thomas shook his head. "I doubt she needs to see me right now. She told me..." He grabbed the letter and thrust it into his friend's hand. "My father put the moves on her, and that's why she cut me dead."

Jack's gaze narrowed. "And you didn't know?"

Thomas glared at Jack. "Well, you know, we sat down and planned it..." Realising how childish that outburst sounded, Thomas sighed. "No. I knew nothing until she handed me this. So, I got looking. I found my dad's diary. He hid them all, I guess to make sure nothing self-incriminating could be found." Disgust echoed in every word. How he loathed the knowledge that his father was an even bigger sleaze then he'd learned. "He had Mum hide them, and she did."

"Your mother was a good woman."

"He hit her," Thomas announced. "When I wasn't around. She was scared. I found a journal. She never told anyone about it. Wrote down that her counsellor made her keep it. I think she was planning on leaving Dad, then they had the accident."

Jack stared at him, the moment stretching out, but his eyes glittered with understanding and empathy. "I'm truly sorry, Tom. I didn't know. I would have done something if I had."

Jack's sympathy was too much right now, because the bubble in Thomas' chest kept growing, threatening to suffocate him. "Yeah. Look, I need to do something. Keep busy. I was thinking, we saved one family, and there's bound to be others who'd benefit from being here. Young families, hiding out. We could..."

"That's why I came. Our radio operator got word of some families hiding out near Tirrogerren. They were safe until recently. There's been incursions. The big bastards are getting closer. We can help them if we can get to them quickly."

Thomas squared his shoulders. "Tell me everything you know."

CHAPTER 1

Kelly grunted and lifted the net. Times out here on the water seemed almost interminable, so she'd taken to fishing further afield. Today, she'd crossed the channel and looked beyond to the empty mainland. The sound of the wind, the rock of the boat. If she closed her eyes, she could almost think that nothing had changed.

"And yet, you'd be wrong." The tang of salt settled on her tongue, and she reached for the water bottle, taking a swig to wash away the taint.

A sound caught her attention, a flash of colour following.

It sounded like, "Help!"

Sitting up, Kelly squinted.

A child, maybe ten or so, sprinted down onto the beach, while the harsh dirge of the undead echoed.

"Over here," bellowed Kelly, waving her arms frantically. "Swim here."

The child looked up and dove into the water, arms churning with untutored moves.

Out into the sunshine lurched three large creatures. "Shit!" She hit the button to start the motor while screaming, "Swim faster!"

The child reached the side of the boat as the first creature lumbered into the water.

Kelly pulled the child aboard then returned her attention to the controls, and the boat shot forward. "Hold on," she yelled and pulled them away from the beach, aware of the frenetic beating of her heart.

Loud, long moments passed before she cut the engines. The child stared at her, face scratched and bruised. "Am I safe?"

"Yes, you are. But what are you doing out there on your own?"

The girl shrugged. "It's how I live. Mum and Dad are zombs, and I live where I want. Do what I want and find what I can to survive."

Her mouth must have been hanging open at the belligerence in the child's voice. "On your own?"

"Yeah? And so what?"

"They nearly caught you."

"Nearly, but not quite. Hey, this is a nice boat. Where do you live?" The little girl cocked her head to the side.

"On the island. But if you've got no parents, how do you survive?"

The girl's face shuttered. "I get by."

"My name is Kelly. What's your name?"

"Why do you want to know?"

The girl was cagey and angry. Just like Kelly had been in those early days after Jack's dad. She'd need to tread carefully if she wanted to help the girl. "Because I can help you. I could take you to the island, and you could be safe. Go to school and so on."

The girl blinked. "There's no schools. You're lying." It was as if a chink of hunger had opened, and Kelly wondered what kind of background the girl had before today.

"There are. We've got teachers, and nurses, doctors, and police. Babies too. There's tons of houses and, best of all, no zombies."

The girl's face became bland, but the need to know more was evident in her eyes. "I could go there?"

Kelly nodded slowly. "You sure could. If you wanted to."

"You're not one of those pervs, are you? Picking up kids and—"

Laughter shot from Kelly's mouth. "No. I'm not a perv. I'm just a fishing woman who saw a kid in trouble. I want to help you if you'll let me." She softened the words, having seen the girl flinch when she'd laughed.

"Why?"

Kelly blinked. "Because I can. Because that's what most people would do."

The girl grunted. "Jessica. My name's Jessica, but no one uses it these days." She shrugged thin shoulders in the misshapen t-shirt. When Kelly looked down, she saw that the girl wore no shoes, and blood pooled at her feet.

"We should get your feet cleaned up and bandaged."

Jessica looked down. "Oh. I didn't feel it."

Holding in a sigh, Kelly wondered if the girl was living on nerves, but refrained from speaking. "I've got a first aid kit here. Sit down and I'll get you cleaned up. Have you had something to eat today?"

"Food? I found a tin this morning. I think it was fish, but it tasted yucky, so I didn't finish it."

"I've got a beef stew here or some sandwiches if you'd rather."

"Like, home-made?" Jessica's eyes shone, then she shut down the eagerness, and a layer of cynicism settled on her features. "Sure," she grunted. "So long as it doesn't leave you short."

Jessica clearly wanted to appear tough, and Kelly felt the burning of tears. At least this time it's not self-pity.

Kelly reached down to the large bag at her feet and drew out the heater dish and cutlery, then handed them to the child. "Put your feet on this," she said and dragged over a bucket. "Eat, while I see to your feet, then we'll get underway."

The girl ate with gulps and quick snatches, like she'd been starved, and given the sparseness of her frame, that wouldn't be too great a leap of logic. Kelly kept herself quiet and set about washing the deep lacerations on Jessica's feet, wondering the whole time if she wouldn't be best letting a doctor look at them. Since Jack and Thomas' trip to the mainland, they had medical professionals who could do most anything. Except save Dad.

She swallowed the lump which lodged in her throat. Her dad had been living on borrowed time since his heart attack years ago, and without the medication he needed, they all knew there was a chance this might come to pass.

"You're crying. Why?" Jessica inclined her head.

"My dad died recently, and I was thinking about him."

"You said there were no zombies," Jessica accused.

"No. He had a heart attack. Dropped dead in the kitchen, and I found him. It was... horrible."

Jessica nodded. "My mum and dad both died. Dad got sick and bit Mum. She made me run away, 'cause she knew what would happen. I've been on my own since then."

"When was that?" Kelly asked, hoping the girl might tell her more.

"Last winter."

"That's like over a year." Kelly fastened the bandage on Jessica's foot. "You've been alone that long?"

The girl looked away, a sneer on her face, and Kelly knew that attitude. Now wasn't the time to question anything else. "Look, are we going to get moving or what's your plan?"

"Sure. If you're finished eating, come and hop into the chair and we'll head home. I've only got a light catch today, so we'll motor into town and unload."

"And me?"

Kelly bit her lip. "Well, I need to talk to the police. Thomas, he's..." She frowned, wondering how best to attack the situation. "Jack is in charge of the island, and he and Addie, his wife, have twin babies, and another on the way, so you won't be able to stay with them."

"I'm not staying with a guy. I can look after myself if—"

"I don't think Jack would allow that. Maybe... You could stay with me at the cabin? Or someone else might be able to take you in while we settle things."

"You're not so bad. At least, I don't think so. I could stay with you."

Unsure quite how to take that, Kelly smiled. "Well, I have a spare room. We just need to organise you some clothes and get you enrolled in the school. Maybe also a doctor's visit—"

"I don't know about that." Now, for the first time, there was a glimmer of something in the girl's features that pointed to terror.

"He's a nice guy, or there's his wife. She's also a doctor. Just let them check you out, see if there's anything you need, and we can head on over to my home. It's by the sea."

"I like the sea. I spend days there sometimes. I was heading for my usual spot when they found me."

Kelly waited as the girl stood and padded over to the seat. "Fasten up, this goes pretty fast once I'm moving."

Jessica obliged and Kelly restarted the motor, checked the compass, and turned toward the island. The child stayed quiet for the trip, and Kelly used the time to consider the circumstances and what she'd learned. Jack would likely want to talk to the girl, see what information he could gather about the zombies.

***

Thomas watched the boat cleaving through the water. After talking with Jack, he'd thought long and hard, and finally decided that Kelly needed to hear what he had to say. It wouldn't be pretty, but he'd spill his guts. Maybe she'd understand. Maybe she wouldn't, but he needed to tell her what he'd learned. He owed her that much.

Adjusting his sunglasses, he frowned as he scanned the rapidly approaching craft. Two people, not one. "What the…?"

His heart thud, his guts clenched. Someone else? Who?

Jealousy. It wasn't an emotion he would normally attest to, but this was Kelly. The woman he'd loved for a long time. The one he'd thought had done him wrong, until now he knew it was the other way around. His casual disregard for what was before him had been his undoing all those years ago. Had he finally realised it, only to lose her when a second chance was unfurling?

He strode down the jetty as the craft slowed then came to a halt. She slid from her seat, and he watched the precision of her movements. The way she grabbed the lines and fastened the boat spoke of years of practice, as if every action was like a well-oiled routine.

Beside her bobbed another head. Now he could clearly see it was a child. A girl.

He moved swiftly, legs eating up the distance. "Kelly? Who's that?"

The grace of her movements was replaced with a wariness he hated, noting the way her actions became jerky. "Thomas. Hi. This is Jessica. She was being chased by zombies."

"On the island? Where?"

Kelly shook her head. "No. I was near the mainland, looking for fresh fishing grounds and about to set some crab traps, when she headed in my direction. She was being chased by big zombies. Like, huge. Muscled and without the usual decay."

Thomas frowned. She knew that area was out of bounds, but he kept that thought firmly chained. "I don't…?"

"We need to see Jack, but first Jessica needs to see the doctor."

"What, she's been bitten?" He glanced down at the girl who'd shrunk in beside Kelly, and he noted the way Kelly slid a hand back, as if keeping her shielded. That hurt, cut right through him.

"No. She's hurt her feet, and I want the doctor to look and see if she needs stitches or a tetanus shot."

"I'm not getting a needle," the girl growled.

"We'll see what the doctor says, then we can talk about it, Jessica, okay?" Kelly stated, ushering the girl forward but sliding her on the side away from Thomas.

"Jack needs to know," Thomas ground out, and Kelly nodded.

"He can come to the medical centre then, because that's where we're headed. You can either take us or we'll walk," Kelly declared.

He eyed the boat. "What about the fish?" He knew the hold was refrigerated, but he also knew she didn't like her catch to wait.

Kelly sighed and glanced at him. "It'll wait until the guys get here to unload it. They usually do that for me anyway. Let's go." She ushered the young girl forward and up the jetty.

Thomas felt like a fool. He'd asked the kinds of questions only an idiot would ask, and yet, she'd answered him, all the while letting his fury at the situation simmer. The opportunity to talk about what felt super important mere moments ago had melted like ice-cream in the sun. He felt adrift—a feather on a breeze—and Thomas was discovering he didn't really enjoy that situation.

***

The feel of Thomas' gaze on her back burned. Kelly was still super aware of Thomas. Hell, she'd expected to have been married to him now, if not for the curveballs life had tossed her way.

In a different life, perhaps there may have been a chance for them to overcome all the obstacles, but not now. Hope had faded away, and she was an empty shell. Oh, she put on a good show, so no one really knew the emptiness inside her. Funny, saving Jessica today had done something to awaken emotions long forgotten. Made her feel like she had a chance to change. Kelly bit her lip, feeling the bitter sting of regrets and wishes. She needed to get her head back in the game, because she had a feeling Jessica would test all her limits.

"Where are we going?" Jessica demanded, and Kelly couldn't contain the smile at the girl's query.

"Just across the road here." At the road's edge she checked more from habit than any expectation of traffic. When Jessica made to step out, Kelly stopped her. "We still have cars, so you have to check."

The girl grunted, and Kelly smiled again, then ushered her across the road, after being assured they'd not get run over.

At the door, Kelly stopped. "If you need to talk to the doctor alone, you tell me, and I'll leave. She's honest and nice."

Jessica nodded, and they entered the building. Kelly was well aware that Thomas was trailing them. She stopped at the desk and peered around the corner. "Is there a doctor in?"

Cherie Neilson, one of their newly installed medical team, popped around the corner, smiling, then stopped. "Well, I don't think I've met you before," she said, her gaze on the young girl.

"Jessica, this is Doctor Cherie." Looking at the little woman, Kelly smiled. "Jessica has just joined us. She was escaping some nasties when I found her on a beach. Her feet are a little the worse for wear, and I'd feel a whole heap better if you'd give her a quick check-up."

Cherie nodded, her short hair only moving slightly with the action. "Of course. Well, Jessica, it's up to you if Kelly joins us—"

"I'm not going in without her."

Cherie's gaze clashed with Kelly's. "Okay. That's not an issue. Come through to my room and we'll start with your feet, shall we?"

Once Jessica was perched on the side of the bed, Kelly took a chair beside the desk and Cherie got to work.

"Before we begin, I have to get some information," Cherie said. "I know your name is Jessica. Do you have a last name?"

Jessica answered the questions, including her age—ten in three weeks, as it turned out—and where she'd lived. Some questions she had ready answers for, but others like vaccinations she couldn't answer. Cherie simply smiled and said they'd see what they could find out and the consultation rolled on.

Finally, Cherie reached out and unbandaged Jessica's feet. "Well, that's nasty. Kelly's done a good job with cleaning the wounds, but I'm going to prescribe some antibiotic pills for you to take. They're as much a precaution because we don't know what you might have stepped in. This one," she said and reached into a drawer, "is a broad spectrum. Take one tablet three times a day, with food."

Jessica screwed up her nose. "I don't like taking pills. Mum used to say..." Then she stopped.

Cherie moved closer. "It's really hard as an adult to lose everything you know. I can't even imagine how hard it is for you. If you want to talk about your parents, I doubt anyone would have an issue with that. Sometimes, the talking alone will make you feel better."

Jessica's chin wobbled. "But they're dead."

Cherie nodded. "Yes, they are. But that doesn't have to mean forgotten. We can keep them alive in our memories and thoughts."

To Kelly, it was as if Cherie was talking directly to her, and the wave of grief she'd ignored since finding Jessica almost swamped her.

Cherie turned now and looked at Kelly. "I heard about your father, Kelly. If you need anyone...?"

Kelly could only nod, because right now, they were here to focus on Jessica's needs.

"I mean it, Kelly. And if you need a top up of your script—"

"I'm all good. Thanks, Cherie. If there's nothing else?"

"Well. I have a couple of delicate questions to ask." She turned back to Jessica. "You want Kelly here for them?"

The girl tensed up. "What?"

"I know living on your own is difficult. I need to ask if anyone tried to take advantage of you. Sexually."

The girl paled. "Nooooo.... Why?"

"Well, Jessica, girls on the streets and unprotected are open season to those with sick and twisted needs. If you have been touched, or more, then sometimes you need help. Someone to talk to, medical exams, stuff like that."

"There was this one guy. He tried, but I bit him, and kicked and scratched. I ran away. He told me I had to touch him. You know, like down there." She pointed to her midsection.

Cherie nodded, her face a mask. "Did he hurt you?"

Jessica shook her head slowly. "No, he just tried to touch me, and I kicked him. Between the legs, really hard, like my dad always said to do. He screamed like a girl." She sniggered then subsided with a long, drawn-out sigh. "I ran away and hid."

"You did well," soothed Cherie while Kelly fumed. No girl should have to deal with these kinds of predators, and now especially, lone girls were a serious target.

If only you could do something about it.

A quick glance at Jessica reminded Kelly that she was. On a small scale.

But is it enough?

Kelly rose from the seat, uncomfortable with the mental argument her brain had decided was the way to sort this out. "Thanks for seeing us at such short notice, Cherie. I've got fish in the hold, so Jessica and I should get going. If you want some, follow me down to the boat and I'll load you up before the guys empty everything out."

Cherie laughed and screwed up her nose. "I'm not a big seafood eater, so I'll pass today. Next time though, just drop me off some fish and maybe crabs?"

"You've got it," called Kelly as she and Jessica left the room. "So, that wasn't so bad, was it?" She glanced down at the girl's hands. "Good, you've got your pills. We'll head home and you can have a rest while I moor the boat and clean it, then I'll change, and we'll come into town and meet with Jack."

CHAPTER 2

Thomas seethed. Kelly and the girl—Jessica—had taken off in the time he'd spent making his way up to his office to let the sergeant know what had happened and returning to the jetty. He'd seen the boat chugging off into the sunset.

"Bloody hell," he grouched, "you could have waited for me."

He climbed into his aging police car, and it rocked as he settled into the driver's seat. The car moved down the street and he turned, heading for Jack's office. "Might as well kill two birds with one stone," he muttered.

In truth, he felt the need for a buffer because his every interaction with Kelly since she'd handed him that letter had scoured him, and he guessed more than likely both of them. Even now, on the jetty, the first flush of jealousy was followed by fury that she'd put herself in danger to save the child. Not that he'd have done anything different, but still...

Pulling up at Jack's, he was pleased to see the newer model vehicle sitting outside. Dragging himself from the car, he loped to the door and entered the building. "Jack? Addie?"

"In the office," called Addie, and he followed the hallway to the small office area at the rear.

In the room outside, a playpen was set up and two crawling

toddlers raised themselves up and babbled at him. "Hey Leanne and Fiona. Keeping busy, huh?"

Addie popped her head around the corner. "Come on in. We're looking at the finalised housing allocations." She grinned widely. "It'll be good to have your input too."

She laid her hand on her rapidly expanding belly as she spoke, and when she hugged him, he would have sworn there was a decided pump to his belly. "Was that...?"

"He or she is active today. Punching me black and blue." But she laughed as if it were the highlight of her day.

"Yeah, I'll bet." He followed Addie into the office, lowered himself into the chair beside her, and looked across the desk at his friend, Jack. "We have a problem. Kelly went too far out. Actually, she was basically on the mainland, and while she was there, a child turned up, being chased by zombies. She saved the girl and brought her back here."

"A child. Oh no!" Addie's mouth nearly dropped to her chest. "Is she okay?"

"Oh yeah. I guess she's in the region of around nine or ten? By the looks of it, she's been on her own for some time. Kelly's taken the girl home with her. Jack, she's putting herself in danger by leaving the safety of the channel."

Jack watched him. "While I agree, I'm pleased to hear she helped the child. A girl, you said?"

"Jessica," Thomas corrected. "But Kelly knows the boundaries. You need to talk—"

"She's a big girl. Old enough to make decisions for herself," Jack interrupted.

"Jack..."

"Look, immaterial, she's out there, and she did the right thing as far as she's concerned. I'm not going to rake her over the coals for saving a child's life." His friend sighed. "I know you're struggling and want to keep her safe, but your situation isn't one I'm going to get in the middle of. You need to talk to her."

Thomas hated the truths but couldn't argue. *Jack's right. I do need to talk to her, to clear the air.*

Clearing his throat, Jack stared at him. "I do think we should pay a visit though. Find out more about this girl and see what needs to be done. Addie, fancy a drive? It'll take your mind off these lists, and the girls would no doubt like a chance to stretch their legs."

Addie rose up. "I'll grab them—"

"No, not when you've got two strong men who can't resist the wiles of our daughters. Rest your back for a while, sweetheart."

Addie smiled at Jack, her features soft and lover-like, and Thomas had to look away, rather than act the voyeur, especially given that they radiated the intention to kiss. He moved back into the main room, picking up one of the twins. A tiny necklace with an 'F' informed him she was Fiona. "Come on, kiddo. Your parents are doing the suck-face thing, and you're too young to watch." It was a moment of remembered mirth, the comments about other couples kissing a left-over from their teen years.

The sound of sniggering drew his attention, and he looked up to see Jack watching from the doorway. "One day, my friend, you'll join the ranks of the 'suck-face brigade.' Then I'll remind you."

Jack scooped up Leanne, who giggled at the grunting sounds he made as he did, and Addie appeared with the ever-present bag of baby paraphernalia slung over her shoulder.

"Ready to go?" Jack asked.

Thomas nodded and they trooped out, Addie locking the building while Jack placed the two little girls into their car seats. "I'll follow," Thomas muttered, aware as always that space was limited with the large seats filling the backseat.

"Suits me." Jack grinned. "Then I can talk dirty to my girls."

Thomas rolled his eyes and headed for his own car. He'd go on ahead and meet Kelly before Jack and his entourage appeared.

The drive was silent, though not soothing. His mind whirred at a million miles with the 'what could have gone wrong' scenarios only his brain could conjure up.

What if the engine failed?

What if the zombie could swim?

What if the girl had been bitten and didn't realise she was going to turn?

Every thought was more horrifying than the last so that by the time he turned into the driveway, his guts were tied into knots, roiling on a greasy sea.

He got out of his car, slammed the door, and stalked to the front of the cabin. Knocked and waited. Silence.

Jack's car pulled up beside his and the two adults climbed out. "What's wrong, Thomas?" called Addie.

"She's not here."

"Have you tried the mooring?" Jack prompted. "She's probably cleaning the boat down before heading inside."

Thomas turned and stomped toward the sands, but not before he heard Addie asking, "What's wrong with Thomas?"

He scowled but swallowed the 'nothing' answer. He'd sound like a petulant bear... which was probably the most accurate description of his mindset at this point, he concluded morosely. It wasn't that he didn't want Kelly to get on with her life, he just...wished he were part of it.

He crested the sandy hillock and looked down to the mooring. She and the girl were hosing the boat deck and using a broom to clear the fish scales and slime from the wood. Taking a moment, he let his gaze roam over her form. Noting that she was even more toned than he'd remembered, and the way her actions were swift and well-practiced.

In the past, she'd given up her dreams of interior design and come home to help her father, at first claiming it was because of the heart attack. Later, she'd never raised what she wanted to be again, and he wondered if she'd been hiding in the aftermath of his father's actions. Yet another possible revelation to shake his world. *For a self-assured man of the world, you've been a dimwit.*

He should have known, seen the changes in her. The way she kept her distance.

Now, he moved forward and down, heading to the pontoon. "Need help?"

She whirled, wobbling with surprise, and lost her footing. He reached out, caught her as she fell. "Damn it, Thomas, what the hell were you thinking sneaking up on me?"

"Sorry," he muttered and looked in the direction of the youngster watching them. "Everything okay? No unpleasant surprises?" Like, will she turn into a zombie? The question sat on the tip of his tongue, but he swallowed it.

"No. But you can turn off the tap. We're finished here, then we're heading inside. I need a shower, and so does Jessica."

He reached over, found the faucet head, and turned it, the water flow stopping almost immediately. "Great, except Jack and Addie are here with the girls."

"What?" she squeaked. "But I'm filthy."

"We don't mind," called Addie. "Besides, I brought cake!"

Jessica's eyes grew round. "Cake?"

"Carrot with cream cheese icing. I'll put the kettle on while you guys shower quickly. By the time you're out, hot drinks will be ready and slices too." Addie shooed both females up the crest and off to the cabin.

Jack hung behind with Thomas. "I see what you mean," Jack said. "There's some discussions to be had."

"The first being what to do with the kid," muttered Thomas.

"I don't see why, if they're both willing, Jessica couldn't stay with Kelly. She's got the room, and she's alone. Jessica too is used to being alone, so it makes sense. One person for each situation," Addie suggested.

Thomas remained quiet. Feeling like he really didn't have a say in the situation irked him badly.

"Good points, Addie. Let's get in there, and you can sit down. We'll take care of the babies if you want a rest?" Jack's tone was full of concern, and Thomas wondered if she was experiencing issues with the pregnancy. After all, Fiona and Leanne were barely a year old, and she had another one baking. Tom picked up a baby, snuggling her against his chest.

"No, I'm all good, so you can stop cocooning me. Everything's fine." And she appeared to glow to Thomas' uninitiated view.

"I'm just worried." Jack's hand captured Addie's hand yet again, and their fingers twined together in the age-old symbol of togetherness. His actions reminded Thomas of all he'd lost.

Thomas followed the couple to the door.

Addie dropped the large bag, and Jack removed a mixture of toys.

The babies settled on the floor, mouthing on the toys while nattering away in their garbled baby language.

"Does it ever get boring?" The words shot from Thomas' mouth before he could think.

Jack blinked. "No. Too much to do and too much to look forward to." In the air hung the unspoken 'you'll understand some day' that it seemed most married couples trotted out.

"Oh Thomas, there's still a chance, if you're willing to take it," Addie said, and Thomas looked at her.

"There's... It's complicated, Addie. Let's just leave it at that."

"What's complicated, Tom?" Kelly's voice echoed from the doorway, and he blushed, the heat scorching.

"Just stuff."

Kelly's mouth tightened and her eyes narrowed, but she didn't say anything. Has she worked out Addie was talking about them?

"Oh, I was just telling Thomas that you two would make a great couple," Addie enthused, sliding the hot drinks to the tabletop.

Thomas wanted to sink through the floor. He had no interest in embarrassing Kelly like that, and clearly Addie's words weren't sitting well with her.

"Thanks for making the tea," Kelly answered and lowered herself into her chair. "To be honest, Addie, I really don't want to talk about that right now. The situation that needs to be considered is Jessica."

The girl came through the doorway, wearing an old dress of Kelly's that he remembered well.

"Jessica, would you like a tea or some hot chocolate?" Addie asked. "I spied a pack here on the side."

The girl's eyes brightened. "Do you have marshmallows too?"

Kelly shook her head. "No. But we could see if there's some at the store later today. I have to go grab some food anyway."

"Well, it's been like forever, so chocolate would be great." Then, as if she realised what she'd said and how open she'd been, the girl withdrew before his eyes. She sat down at the table, furthest away from everyone except Kelly.

Addie made the drink and placed it in front of her, and Jack cleared his throat. "I'm Jack, and that's my wife Addie. The babies are Leanne and Fiona. You know Kelly and Thomas."

Jessica nodded, circling her fingers around the warm cup.

"We're glad you're here, but we have to sort out what we're going to do with you. Now, we can't have youngsters like you living by yourself. It's just not safe, but finding you a home..." Jack shrugged.

"She can stay with me, if she's comfortable," Kelly offered.

The girl looked at Thomas, Jack, and Addie. "I get a choice?"

"Within reason," Jack answered.

"I don't know any of you, but Kelly saved me. Not that I was in difficulty or anything." The girl's words were spoken with more than a hint of 'go on, argue it.'

He felt Kelly stiffen and glanced her way. Her features didn't betray her, unlike the Kelly of old. Back when they'd been boyfriend and girl-friend her every emotion had shown on her face. It was one of the things that first drew him, the innate honesty about her. Now, it was as if she guarded the very essence of herself and her emotions. That's so odd. She always used to be transparent. It reminded him that years had passed by, and he'd kept enough distance to not notice the changes taking place.

It took every ounce of willpower to not reach out, to touch her and remind her that emotions weren't something to hide. Was I part of this change? Thinking back, Thomas remembered Addie and Jack's wedding. The happiness, and the way she'd become friends with Addie, and it made him wonder now, had it been real, or just a façade? Confusion filled him. It was an emotion he despised.

"Thomas?" Addie's voice broke through the veil surrounding him.

"Huh? What?" The words were little more than a croak.

"Are you okay, Tom?" Jack stared at him, and once again the red tide of heat flushed over him.

"Yeah, I was just thinking about something. What's wrong?"

Jack stared for an instant longer. "Kelly and Jessica out here. It's a concern. We could move them into town, but Kelly was saying the boat needs to be moored here. So perhaps you could come stay, for now?"

He looked at Kelly, noted the glint in her eyes, which was probably the only giveaway that she didn't like that plan at all.

"Well, I could, but I'm not sure Kelly would be comfortable with that. Besides, it's not as if there are any zombies left—"

"That we know of," finished Jack.

"They can swim," offered Jessica, and all eyes swivelled to the young girl.

"What?" Thomas didn't even bother to hide his shock. If they can swim—

"How the hell do you know that?" demanded Jack while Addie reached out and grabbed his hand, her face white.

"I've never seen that," added Kelly.

The girl nodded. "The big ones. They're new. Faster. Hungrier, and they can swim. I saw it just the other day. Makes me think something is happening and they're changing."

Silence reigned as the shock settled on all. They'd been in a bubble of safety, thinking that here on the island with the bridge gone, they'd been safe. Now? The game had changed.

CHAPTER 3

Kelly settled herself on the bank, looking out, scanning the water for signs of the undead coming in their direction.

Jessica's announcement had ended the happy atmosphere and left them with more questions than answers. Jack had ushered Addie and the babies from the building as fast as he could, and Kelly guessed he'd be calling a meeting of the elders to discuss the very unwelcome news that their safety was once again jeopardised. Thomas had decamped as well, while Jessica had seemed wholly unconcerned.

"And why would she? She's a child," Kelly told herself.

Kelly and Jessica would need to make the run into the township soon for food, except right now, it seemed like such an effort. One she just couldn't face. So, instead she'd come out to commune with the water and hoped to come up with something useful to offer.

"You know, I know you're upset." Jessica's voice echoed behind her, and Kelly turned.

"Not with you. It's just... We spent so much time making this place into a safe zone. Now, with the news you've shared, it's not so safe anymore." Kelly patted the ground beside her in invitation to the girl.

Jessica plopped herself onto the sand beside Kelly, her face screwed up. "But you've got guns and boats."

Kelly laughed at the innocence of Jessica's words. If only the world was as simple as Jessica suggested. But life—not just existence—was more than survival, a fact she'd clearly forgotten until recently, it seemed.

"Guns and boats, yes, but not unlimited fuel. Nor are there enough people to keep our entire coastline safe. The people here? They're looking for safety. Security."

"So, they could still reach us then?"

Kelly shrugged. "I don't know. We need more information, like how far they can swim, how long they can survive the water."

"But the sharks will kill them."

God, Kelly wished she had Jessica's optimism. "Maybe, and maybe not." She looked back to the horizon. "We just don't know enough."

"You're going back?" Jessica questioned.

Kelly turned and smiled. "No. But I do have things to do. Like enrol you in school and get you some clothes that fit."

There was no way on earth she was going to admit that tomorrow, once Jessica was safely at the school, she was going out on her vessel to see what more she could learn. Jessica needed safety and a future, while Kelly had nothing else to lose.

She stood up and offered the girl a hand. "Come on. We need to make the run into town, get clothes for you and food. We'll drop past the school and get you enrolled. What subjects did you like?"

Jessica answered her questions as they headed for the car, and Kelly wasn't sure if she believed Jessica didn't know what she planned. At the store, Jessica picked up underwear and shoes, jeans and t-shirts, a couple of pairs of shorts, and a hairbrush. "Mum would have had a cow if she saw my hair."

Kelly smiled. "I'm no hairdresser, but I think we can sort that rat's nest out for you."

On the way back with groceries, Kelly pulled into the school. The bell rang as they parked, and Jessica watched the kids streaming out.

"Don't they know about the zombies?" the girl asked.

"Well, sure. We've had some here, but they feel safe. And as for what you do know, they don't, so don't scare them with tales until we have more information."

The girl stared at her. "But they should know," Jessica argued.

"When and if it's necessary, then the islanders will come together, and the news will be shared. But not now, today, or tomorrow. Jack and Thomas are no doubt coming up with a plan." Just as she was, Kelly thought.

"Alright," Jessica agreed, though through gritted teeth. "But you're going to have to say something before the zombs get here."

Kelly ushered Jessica to the office. "Mrs Harsham? I've got a new student for you. Jessica is a recent arrival, and she needs to be enrolled to start tomorrow."

As at the doctors, there were questions of age and what grade, and finally, about a half hour later, they left the school grounds, Jessica lugging a large pile of books, pencils, and other supplies.

"I've got a backpack at home that you can use until we get you one you like."

"Sure," Jessica responded, dumping the books on the backseat. "But how dumb is it that I have to write, not just use a tablet?"

"You didn't write at school?" Kelly was surprised, thinking everyone did that. After all, wasn't that part of the skill learning thing all kids did? They both climbed into the car and Kelly waited while Jessica fastened her seatbelt.

"No, we haven't done that for ages." There was dripping disgust in Jessica's words. "We used tablet devices, so we didn't have to lug a pile of books." There was such a wealth of disbelief in Jessica's voice that Kelly couldn't contain her laugh.

"Well, there you go. Sadly, everything is the old-fashioned way here. You'll just have to get used to it," she said in a jovial tone.

"Huh. Backwards much?" groused Jessica. "Okay, so what's for dinner?"

Kelly glanced at the girl beside her, surprised at the lightning change of topic. "Uh... We could do fish and chips. I've got to harvest some potatoes, but that might be a nice option?"

"Huh, I could help. I like working in the garden. Gran used to..." Her face screwed up. "I miss Gran and Mum and Dad."

Heart squeezing, Kelly reached out and put her hand on the girl's. "I'm sorry you lost them all. I don't..." What do you say to a kid who's lost everything? Sorry felt lame and useless, but she was. "This whole situation sucks. Like great, big, hairy monkey balls." Then, realising what she'd said, Kelly covered her mouth. "I can't believe I said that," she groaned.

Jessica sniffled a laugh. "Mum used to tell Dad off when he swore, but..." She shrugged. "Nothing will ever be the same again."

"No. But if we only think about the bad stuff, that's all we'll look for, because our brains think that's normal. We have to look for positives, to make our lives better." Take your own advice, Kelly. She'd forgotten the words her counsellor had told her years ago until just now.

"You reckon?"

"A long time ago, a very clever person told me that," Kelly clarified.

"But you don't practice it, do you? Something about you is sad."

Kelly sighed. "That's true. I'd forgotten to focus on the good things, but while I'm still really sad, since my dad died, I need to begin finding positives and good things. Tonight, I'm looking forward to freshly caught fish. I have a nice snapper in the fridge. Have you ever had that before?"

"I don't know. We didn't fish much."

"Hmm, but you'd like to learn?" Kelly wondered if the girl had the whole 'ick factor' girly thing happening.

"Mum didn't like it, so I didn't get to learn. But I like to get outside."

"Good then. We'll have to teach you. I have my old rod in the shed somewhere, and I've got plenty of bait and we can always catch more." The cabin loomed ahead.

"Can we get it out today?"

Kelly shook her head. "No. It's going to take a while, and we have to dig the potatoes, get the fish out of the fridge, and get dinner on. And I'm thinking early bed wouldn't be a bad idea after you get your room set up."

"Aww, really?" In that second, Jessica sounded like every kid Kelly had ever known.

Kelly grinned. "Yep. I may not have a lot of experience with kids in the house, but even I see the sense in this."

The girl climbed from the car, and Kelly helped her carry the piles of items to her spare room.

"I'll grab some sheets. Do you know how to make a bed?" Kelly asked.

"Sure. Mum made me make it every day."

Kelly could hear her grief, but she guessed that having Jessica talk about it was probably healthy.

***

Thomas waited until the school was due to start before heading downstairs and climbing into his car. He'd catch Kelly before the boat went out, he thought.

When he reached the waterfront and climbed over the hillock leading down to the mooring, he realised he'd been too late. It was only after he noted the nets pooled at the side that worry filled his gut. Where had Kelly gone, and why hadn't she taken her nets?

He grabbed the handheld mic from his belt, clicked the button once and waited for the 'yeah' before following up with, "Hey, Jack. Any reason Kelly would have left her nets behind?"

"Fuck. No. She's up to something though." A silence filled the air, before a click, "Addie said she's been asked to pick up Jessica after school, and Kelly reckons she'll be back before dark."

The worry in his gut grew larger and even greasier. The Kelly he'd known years ago would have told him what she was up to, but the woman he now knew was insular. Self-sufficient.

"She's doing something she didn't want us to know, Jack."

"Maybe she's checking something?" Jack's words were hopeful. "Look, she's not an idiot, and she likely has a good reason. Wait until she's back and we can—"

"Fuck that, Jack. The nets are here. I used to come out often enough to know when something is off. She's up to something."

Fury coursed through his veins, because he was sure she was doing something that was dangerous. Just look at yesterday when she'd gone too close to the mainland and picked up the kid. Not that he wanted anything bad to happen to Jessica, but Kelly wasn't supposed to be anywhere near the mainland, and now they knew she was going there regularly. What else might she have done or been considering?

The fury warred with terror. What if something happened to her? There was no one able to keep her safe. "Damn it…"

"Tom, there's not much that can be done now. Why don't you come around here and you can talk to Kelly when she arrives to pick up Jessica?"

His muscles were almost jumping out of his skin. "What if in the meantime—"

"Tom, we can't second-guess. You know that. We don't know where she is or what she's up to," Jack tried to calm him.

"Jack—"

"What else is there to do? Think, Tom. You're worried, I can understand that, but what can we do right now?"

Thomas thrust a shaking hand into his hair and looked out to the water. "I don't know."

"Exactly. We talk to Kelly. Find out what she's doing. I'm not sure we can stop her, but maybe we can send someone with her. Mitigate the danger."

Thomas grunted. "Maybe." He gave a last scan of the horizon. "I've got a few things I want to talk to you about anyway."

"Like what?"

"I'll talk with you when I see you, okay? I'm coming back into town. Are you in the office?"

"Yes. Addie has a doctor's appointment and I've got the girls, so if you want to pop in, feel free." Jack sounded puzzled by his request, and Thomas knew he'd be downright shocked by what he had to say.

"I'll be there soon." Thomas clicked off the communication device and slid it onto his belt before turning and heading back to his car. "I'm not going to miss you, not one bit," he muttered as the car creaked and groaned.

The car started without a hiccup, and he turned around, driving onto the road, the whole time his mind considering how he'd deliver his announcement. On arriving at the office, he parked, climbed out, and locked the car from habit before he headed for the door. It opened without a sound, and Thomas strode inside.

Jack was at the end of the hallway. "Coffee?"

Thomas nodded and followed him to the kitchen zone. Small, with a tiny fridge, kettle and sink, it wasn't much but had satisfied the needs of the council staff who'd used it prior to the infection sweeping through the inhabitants. Now, Jack and Addie basically ran the building with the odd ex-staff member opening the library two or three mornings a week.

"So, what's on your mind, Tom?"

They made their coffees, and he took a sip. Waited until his friend put down his cup.

"I've resigned from the police." The words were stark, and Jack stared at him.

"Why?"

"Look, the situation here on the island is stable, or as stable as it's likely to get. It seems to me we need something different than what we had before. Yes, we need policing, but the sergeant has that controlled. I feel I'd be more use to you scouting and assisting with defence and so on. I'm a crack shot, as you know." His guts jittered, even though he knew everything he said had merit. "I can pick and train others, and we can form a mini defence force, if you will. Call us the militia or even just armed civilians, I don't care, but until we start to consider how we defend ourselves, especially now that we know they can swim, we leave ourselves open to attack."

Jack swore. "Fuck. I hadn't really thought of that. I mean..."

"You've got your hands full making sure everything works. And let's be brutally honest, you're not trained to think that way."

"Neither are you," Jack pointed out.

Thomas inclined his head. "Not really, no. But I can see the dangers. I have an idea how we can make this work, but we need bodies. Trained manpower. Lookout towers. We need to put into place anything that will protect us, Jack. I need you to make the case though, to talk the rest into it."

"I need to think—"

"We're running out of time. They can swim. How far, we don't know, but that changes the game as we know it. Think, Jack." He pointed to the two toddlers on the floor. "Those girls there could be attacked if the zombies make it to the island. Will you place them in danger?"

"No fucking way," growled Jack.

"That's what I mean. We need to act now."

Jack nodded. "How soon?"

Understanding the question, Thomas answered, "Today's my last day. Tomorrow I'm on my own. We need to sit down, make a plan, and put it to the islanders. As soon as we can."

Thomas watched, aware his friend needed time to digest what he'd thrown at him, and waited as Jack sipped his coffee, considering what he'd said, before they silently made their way to the seating area.

Both men had just settled in when the door opened again and Addie came whirling in, her face shining. "Honey! Cherie wants to do an ultrasound tomorrow."

Jack half-rose.

"No, nothing is wrong. But she could see the sex of the baby, and well, I know you're dying to know," Addie enthused.

"But everything is okay?" Jack's tone took on an 'OMG' quality.

"Yes. The little one is bouncing and healthy. Everything is getting ready for a normal delivery sometime in about two months."

Jack swiped an unsteady hand over his brow, and Thomas wondered, for the first time, if he'd ever feel that jagged balance of excitement and terror at the thought of a baby. His mind cast to Kelly.

"That's great, but did Kelly say where she was heading?" Thomas asked.

Addie shook her head. "No. Just that Jessica would need someone to pick her up after school. I said I would because I was going to head home early anyway. The girls can have a nap, and so can I, while Jessica putters around with homework and stuff."

"Huh," Thomas grunted.

"Is she in danger?" Addie's voice turned quiet.

"I don't know. She took off, leaving the nets off the boat. It's like she was planning on heading somewhere that didn't involve fishing." Thomas waited a beat, hoping that anything else Addie knew would be triggered by his words.

Addie's eyes widened, and she slumped into a seat beside Jack. "I know she's bright and bubbly, but I get the feeling she shows us the 'her' she wants us to see, not necessarily what's going on inside, you know?" Addie bit her lip. "If she listened to what Jessica was saying, she might have taken the boat out to..." Her voice trailed away, and Thomas realised Addie was coming to the same conclusion he had. "She wouldn't do something that dangerous, would she?" Her hands clasped around Jack's free hand.

"Maybe. Possibly," he answered.

"I think I'm going to be sick," croaked Addie, then she rose unsteadily and tottered toward the bathroom.

"You're thinking that too, right, Jack?"

Jack nodded. "I do."

Thomas sighed, rubbing his hair with his free hand. "I think she went out there to get the answers to our questions. Only we don't know where that is, otherwise I'd be on my way out there." His hand curled into a ball.

Jack shook his head. "That alpha male shit won't make her feel better about you."

Sipping his coffee, Thomas grunted in agreement. "Maybe not, but she's...she's still important to me." That admission is like a razor blade slicing through my skin.

"Then you need to tell her that."

Emotions, dark and hot, flared inside him at Jack's words. "Yeah. But how?" He looked at the ceiling, but there weren't any answers there. "I want her back in my life. I want that chance, but I can't help feeling that my father's actions and my reaction have caused more harm than I can overcome."

"How?"

"She's changed, Jack. The woman I see now is wary. She guards herself and her emotions. All we see is what she wants us to see, not the real Kel, like Addie said. Before, she couldn't have told a lie to save herself, but now, she hides stuff. Like going off by herself. Before she would never have gone anywhere by herself. Remember those summers when we hunted in a pack? If I wasn't there, it was Josie or Lena."

"And they're both gone," Jack added as Addie returned.

"What's going on?"

"We're talking about Kelly. The Kelly we went to school with. How she was the life of the party, the girl everyone wanted to know," Jack explained.

"She's not like that now. I mean, she's friendly but—"

"Since her dad died, she's more alone than not. The house is the most remote on the island," Thomas added.

"Then maybe we need you up there. To keep an eye on the coastline," Jack murmured.

"I'm not going to railroad her, mate. That's not how—"

"No, Tom. Think about what I'm saying. It's remote. She and Jessica are alone up there. What if the zombies do attack? Your theory has merit," said Jack.

"What theory?" questioned Addie.

"Tom reckons if the zombies can swim, we need a militia on lookout. We need to be aware of the coastline and patrol it aggressively. He's resigned from the police, and I'm going to form a plan with him, take it to a community meeting. Island-wide. Everyone needs to know."

Addie watched Jack and nodded. "That makes a lot of sense. Alright then, maybe we should start planning the when and where."

CHAPTER 4

The sun was setting as Kelly chugged the boat to the mooring. Her trip hadn't answered any questions. But then, that would be expecting a miracle on the first go, wouldn't it?

As she came along side, she cut the engines and threw the ropes, then sorted out what she needed to carry off and scurried up the side of the dune separating sea from land.

The keys to the car sat in her pocket, and a look at the setting sun had her scowling. "I should have come back earlier," she muttered to herself.

It was easy to forget that right now it wasn't just herself that she needed to think about. She had Jessica too, and she'd promised to be back well before nightfall. A promise she'd failed to keep.

Sprinting to the car, she tugged the door open and slid inside. She slipped the key into the ignition and jerked the car around, heading for the road.

"At least I don't have to worry about traffic," she growled.

It was a quick trip to Addie and Jack's, and pulling up outside, she hurried from the car, through the large gates and up to the house. The steps at the front of the old Queenslander were quickly overcome, and she peered inside to see Thomas, Jessica, and Jack playing with the babies. The scent of food told her it was nearly dinnertime, and once more she felt guilty for her late arrival.

"Sorry, I got held up," Kelly called as she stepped inside.

Thomas looked up, and on his face, she read frustration and anger. "Kelly. You're back."

"Thought you'd be here earlier," whined Jessica, and Kelly bit her lip.

"Sorry, I tried to get back earlier," she muttered.

"Huh," Jessica replied, clearly put out.

"Oh, you made it. I've got dinner cooking. It's not exciting, but I thought five-spice pork chops and veggies would do the job tonight. I've cooked enough for all of us, so don't make out that you need to run away, Kelly." Addie carried plates, and Jack rose to take the load off his wife. "Jessica, if you could help me, that would be fantastic," called Addie, and a clearly reluctant Jessica stood to assist her.

"Kelly, where did you go today?" questioned Jack.

She glanced at him. "Out looking at the fish shoals. We need an idea of where the best grounds are." The lie came easily, but she'd had the day to practice.

"Bullshit," Thomas responded. "You went to the mainland, didn't you?"

She considered another lie, then shrugged. "Okay, so what if I did?"

"Why?" Jack asked.

Kelly blinked. "What?"

"I need to know why, Kelly. Why did you go back there?" Jack pushed, and she stared at him.

Long seconds passed as she weighed up the best answer to give. It was a struggle to explain the feeling that had overtaken her, what she'd realised now but never before.

"Look, Jessica said they can swim, right? We know there's new zombies. Stronger and bigger, and it appears they aren't like the other slower shufflers. I mean, they're dangerous too, but these? They're different." She turned a circle, thinking about the best way to share the thoughts that crowded her mind. "The ones that came after Jessica? They're still muscled, without the same kind of decay we're used to. Different, like, as if they're evolving." Before anyone could say anything, Kelly stilled her movements, then held up a hand. "I know how stupid that sounds. Evolution, right? These are freaking zombies. But still, I got to thinking if Jessica got away, there are probably others there too. Girls and boys needing help." She shrugged. "I need to do something useful, Jack. I need to feel like I matter." The words slipped out.

"You do matter, Kel. To me." Thomas' voice filled her with something she didn't dare examine. If she named it 'hope' and she was wrong, it would likely destroy her.

Turning in his direction, Kelly stared at him, drinking in his presence. He stood there, waiting for her to respond.

Addie called, and he retreated for a moment. Kelly sucked in an unsteady breath, although intensely aware that Jack was watching her. She struggled to find her equilibrium, but it hadn't returned when Thomas reappeared, holding a plate piled high with steaming meat.

Their gazes met. "I..." she started.

"It's okay, Kelly. We can talk about it later, but you do matter."

Tears burned her eyes at Thomas' words.

"And on that thought, Thomas should follow you home and maybe stay at the cabin," Jack said, and Kelly stiffened at his blunt words.

Kelly whirled around, pointed her finger at Jack. "No."

"He resigned from the police force. We need a militia to patrol the island, and he's taking charge," Addie explained.

Kelly stilled. Militia? Were they expecting a fight? An invasion? "We're in danger?"

"If what you're saying—and I'm not discounting anything you've told us—is correct, then yes, Kelly. There's danger to the whole island. If the zombies make it here, the big buggers? They'll kill us. All of us. Including the babies."

The oxygen in her lungs fled. Babies. Children. Innocent lives. "We can't let that happen, Jack. Something has to be—"

"That's why we need a militia. A body of people aware and on the lookout. We need towers to watch from, armed personnel. We need to protect ourselves," Thomas offered.

"But the bridge..." she whispered.

"If they can swim, no one is safe," Addie said.

"We should eat while the food is hot," Jack muttered. "Take some time to think over what we know, then we can talk and plan."

They moved in silence, finding a chair at the table, with Jessica squeezed in between Kelly and Addie, and the men took the empty spaces with a baby on either side. The meal could have been sawdust for all the notice Kelly paid. The act of cutting, chewing, and swallowing stole most of her conscious thought. It wasn't that she was actively ignoring the issue, more that her brain couldn't cope and shut down as a coping mechanism.

When the meal was over, she still felt lost and each movement mechanical and stiff.

"Kelly," Thomas called her name, and she glanced in his direction. "Let me take you and Jessica home."

She wanted to say no, but couldn't. Instead, Kelly nodded her assent, and the quiet party of three left the house.

***

Thomas hated the silence. He hated the look of fear on Kelly's face. And Jessica, as if picking up on the gravity, also remained quiet. He wasn't a father, but he'd dealt with enough juveniles to know she'd read the emotional temperature of the vehicle and wisely kept silent.

He wanted to thank her for that, but now somehow didn't quite seem like the time.

He pulled into the driveway, Kelly's car—a newer model sedan— coming to a gentle halt beside the cabin. He knew there was a garage around the back, but considered that for tonight, the salt air wouldn't do too much damage.

He waited as the two females climbed from the car, Jessica hauling an old backpack he remembered well, then he climbed out too. They followed him to the door, and he slid the key Kelly handed him into the lock, and it opened, then the three entered.

"Jessica, you should head to bed," Thomas said quietly.

The girl nodded, glanced at Kelly, then left the room. Thomas figured she was big enough not to need anything except maybe a glass of water, and that she could get for herself. So, he took Kelly's hand, towed her to the sofa, and waited as she dropped down.

"We're so fucked, Thomas," she muttered.

"Not necessarily. I mean, we've got lots of healthy, strong people. The sergeant has pulled a list of people with licenses for firearms, and we've…I've done an audit of what firearms we think are on the island. We pool the stash of ammunition, train others, and build lookout towers. It can be done. We just need to prioritise how we go about it. Then we set up regular patrols of the shoreline until the towers are erected."

"But how do we know their capabilities? We can dream and think we're safe, hide our heads in the sand. That's what we did before. We fooled ourselves after the bridge—"

"No," Thomas said. "We used the information we had, we believed—"

"This time we don't have information though, do we?" she interjected.

He stopped. "No. No, we don't."

"The only way to get it is to go back out there. To find out just what they are capable of." Her voice grew stronger, as if the determination grew inside her.

"No, Kelly."

"But if they're bigger, faster, and so on, how can we be sure we're safe?" He could hear in her voice and see in her features that Kelly was sure she was on firm ground. "We go with a crew. We take the boat, and we hunt them. You've said in the past that surveillance is key. This time, we use it again, we gather information. If along the way, we can save a few lives…" She shrugged.

"It's dangerous, Kelly." His guts churned, realising that her plan, while light on details, was likely their best hope, and since the death of her father, she was the best captain they'd find.

"I know. We need to find someone who can care for Jessica."

He harrumphed. "We could ask Addie. She might be willing, especially if Jack—"

"No. He has a family, and it's best if he stays behind. If something happens, the island can't afford to lose him."

Thomas considered her words. "You're right, of course."

"I—"

Thomas shook his head, needing to stop her before she said something that would be too much. "No more. Not tonight. You're tired, and so am I."

Her smile was thin. "What do you have to be tired about? You're unemployed."

"Mere technicality." He laughed, and it felt good to be able to banter with her. He'd missed it over the years they'd been apart.

"That was always your favourite line," she muttered, hands clasped tightly in her lap.

"I haven't used it in a long time, Kel."

"Please, Tom. I can't do this. Too much time has passed, and there's been too much hurt for me to even consider an 'us.'" Her voice was thick, as if tears were clogging their escape.

"Kelly, I..." What could he say? Everything that came to mind seemed so lame. He rose and stalked to the door, hands buried in his hair and eyes scrunched up tight. He whirled back. "I didn't see so much. I couldn't understand the gravity of the words until I read that letter. Then it was like a punch to my stomach. I felt... I don't know, lost? Betrayed."

When she reared back, he swore, "Fuck! Not by you. By him. By me. I should have seen. So, I went looking, and I found his fucking diaries, Kel. He wrote it down, the bastard."

She stayed on the sofa, and her face was upturned. He could see the pain clearly, and that speared him.

"I'm so sorry," he said. "I really am. If only you'd told me though. I could have—"

"What? What would you have done, Tom? You were at the academy, and I was still just a kid. In my last year of high school with the nuns the only witnesses. He said he'd tell you I made the move. How eager he'd make me sound..." And on her face, he read the horror and terror she'd felt then and clearly still felt. "It almost broke me. I wouldn't do that to you," she whispered through streaming tears. "I loved you too much."

He moved forward, couldn't contain the visceral demand, and gathered her in his arms. "I would have stood by you, Kelly. You should have given me a chance," he said while she shook in his embrace.

"I... Please, not tonight. I can't do this. I need to settle down. I need to be in control," she whispered.

"No, you don't."

"I do. You don't understand, it's the only way I can cope. The psychologist called it...." And she stopped, like she was fumbling through her mind to recollect the name. "PTSD with control as a coping mechanism."

Squeezing his eyes shut really tight, Thomas recognised the symptoms now. The rigidity of her actions. "I should have known."

She laughed, but the sound was jagged. "No. I'm good at it, Tom."

"You did nothing wrong, Kelly. It's not right."

"Nothing about this situation is right. I'm not right." Kelly tugged from his embrace and stood. "I'll get a blanket and some pillows and sheets and leave them in Dad's room for you."

The need to call her back rose, but he left well alone. Tonight, they'd had enough revelations, and overcoming the wall she kept erecting between them couldn't possibly be fixed in one night.

In that split second, he realised just how desperately he wanted another chance with Kelly. To build a lifetime. If she needed time, he'd give it to her.

CHAPTER 5

Knowing Thomas was in her father's room kept Kelly awake and tossing. It was a torture she could hardly bear. So close and yet the chasm between them couldn't be breached. If she did that, she'd have to relinquish control.

Control. It had been her ally since that fateful day, and now it was a yoke. As the moon rose high through the window, Kelly got out of bed, grabbed her yoga mat, and settled herself on it. A quick meditation might help, she thought. Taking her favourite position, Kelly closed her eyes, shut her mind down long enough to calm the swamping emotions and find a peaceful centre. She inhaled and exhaled, letting the salty tang of the sea air invade her senses.

A little while later a sound alerted her that someone was watching. She opened her eyes to find Jessica hovering.

"Can I talk to you?"

Kelly rose and nodded. "Sure. What's up?"

"You know when you helped me on the beach? You asked me if there were others?"

Kelly nodded again, unsure what Jessica would say next.

"There's a couple of other girls. Ellie and Jane. They're... Well, I'm not sure we're friends, but we hang together. It's safer that way. Last time I saw them, they were scattering. We'd been found by some zombs in the house where we stayed. I don't know if they...you know." The girl looked haunted in the moonlight, and Kelly understood Jessica's fears.

"Okay. You want me to go in and see if I can find them?"

Jessica bit her lip. "Thomas... He won't like it, will he? But I'm safe, and they weren't. Not once the zombs found where we hid. Like, we aren't besties or anything, but you know, we..."

"I'll talk to Thomas. Find a way to get him to agree, and we'll see if we can locate them. But I'll need to know where you hid and any places they may have gone to that were safe. Are there any others?"

Jessica shook her head. "Not kids. Some oldies, but they're not nice to us kids, so we used to prank them."

Kelly popped a hand on the youngster's shoulder. "You were a kid who—"

"Mum would say that's not right, it's a cop-out. We knew better, but I guess it made us feel like we could make decisions. But most of them—the oldies—are gone now. The zombs found them. The big ones, they look for the weak and take them first, like they can plan."

Those words chilled Kelly to the marrow. Like they can plan. If that was the case—

"You need to head to bed. It's a school night. I'm going to make a cup of tea and chill out a little." She waited until the girl returned to her room and hoped Thomas was still a light sleeper.

In the kitchen she filled the kettle, placed it on the hob, and waited for the whistle. As it started its shrill scream, Thomas joined her.

"Something wrong?"

"Have a cup of tea with me," she offered, and grabbed a cup.

"I still prefer coffee." He settled in a seat at the table, his back to the doorway leading to the hall and bedrooms.

She held up the jar, while raising a finger to her lips. Thomas quirked an eyebrow, then spun his head to look over his shoulder. Jessica wasn't there, but Kelly was super aware she was likely still awake, or if she was lucky, drowsing. In the room next door to the kitchen.

"Sure, I can make you a coffee." And she pantomimed the fingers on lips 'be quiet' action again. Once the hot drinks were prepared, she settled at the table and leaned in. Thomas followed suit. "Jessica said there's other kids on the mainland," she whispered. "Two girls, but I don't remember their names. They hung out together."

"Ahh..." he answered.

Kelly shook her head, needing him to understand how the next fact came about. "But she said something else that tweaked. She said they act 'as if they plan.' The zombies."

Thomas reared back. "What?"

"Shh," she entreated. "Jessica needs to sleep, and we need to talk. Because if what she said is correct, our problems are even bigger than we thought."

"We should take this outside then," he growled, and she shivered at the determined timbre of his voice.

"Okay."

They collected their drinks, and Kelly checked through the bedroom door. Satisfied that Jessica was asleep, as she stepped out, she said, "Leave the door open. If she wakes, I don't want her frightened and thinking there's no one here."

"She's asleep?"

"Yeah. Or at least I think so. I mean, I'm not a parent, so working it all out is a bit..." She waved a hand in the air. "Hit and miss, I guess."

They settled down at the small cast iron outdoor setting by the front door.

"Tell me what happened," Thomas said.

"Just now? Or when I found her?"

He growled. "Both."

Kelly giggled. The sound just bubbled up and escaped before she could stop it. "Sorry."

"Don't be, Kelly. Never be sorry for laughing like that. You don't do it nearly enough." In the moonlight he appeared like some kind of god with his sandy coloured hair and chiselled brow.

"You should have been a male model," she whispered then gasped. "Jeez, I didn't mean to say that out loud." A hot blush burned the skin of her face.

He smiled, and she couldn't stop the ripple of lust in her belly. "A male model, hmm? You with that long, blonde hair. Remember you used to twirl it when you were embarrassed?"

"Not now, Tom. Please."

"I'll refrain for now. But sometime soon, Kel, we'll have to sort out this mess between us. And I for one don't intend to wait long."

The words weren't a threat so much as a promise, and the heat she'd been ignoring inside her jumped a little higher. It took every ounce of willpower not to fan herself.

"Tell me about finding Jessica first."

She did, telling him how she'd heard the cry for help, where she'd been sitting, letting the boat float without the anchor. "I mean, I didn't exactly mean to see or hear anything, but I had to help her."

"Of course you did. So, you got her aboard. Then what?"

"They came out of the brush, running. Big and powerful. Bigger than I'd seen before. They didn't stop, and one waded into the water, and I thought he meant to come for me and the boat. I hauled Jessica in and started the engines."

"Anything else?" he asked. "Did they follow you? Did you see them swimming?"

"No. I didn't look back. I was too concerned that it was too dangerous to hang around."

He grunted. "Okay, tonight?"

"I couldn't sleep." No way would she tell him why, that it was all because of his proximity and the feelings he'd reignited inside her. The ones she'd thought long dead and buried. "I decided meditation might be best and had settled in when I heard Jessica in my doorway. She came in and told me about the two girls. The way they, I guess, squatted in this house. Then she said about the oldies. They used to prank them, but she knew it was wrong." Glancing at Thomas, she noted the flattening of his mouth. "They're kids."

"Old enough to know better, but still."

"She regrets it, Tom. Then she said the zombs, as she calls them, picked off the oldies one-by-one. That's when she said it's like they plan."

He sighed, arched his back, and peered at the moon. "Rain coming in the next few days," he muttered, and Kelly waited, knowing this was how he usually thought. Long moments passed before he sat upright again. "We need to find out where they lived. Check there. We need a group of people."

"Including me."

He shook his head. "No. No fucking way, Kel."

"Damn it, I'm still a good shot. Since you, I learned Ju Jitsu, and I'm strong and fast. I can protect myself."

"If you're there, my concentration will be shot."

"Don't use me as an excuse," she said. "I can hold my own. I have more than once already."

He sniffed. "Jack'll have something to say—"

"Bullshit. We moor the boat in a secluded spot, and trust me, there's plenty of places I know. We go in on foot, a small team. We find the location. She'll give me an address or at least the general vicinity. We check for the girls and use it as an opportunity to check out Jessica's claims."

"No."

"Yes," Kelly corrected. "It'll work. You can see it, can't you?"

His jaw tightened, and she knew he was fighting himself. "God damn it!"

"So, we go day after tomorrow, I guess. The quicker the better, but we need a team, supplies. I need to fuel the boat, and I have to bring in a catch tomorrow—" She glanced at her watch. "—today. Enough to tide the islanders over for a couple of days if it takes that long."

A large yawn escaped her.

"Bed sounds good," he said, and once again there was a liquid chocolate timbre to his voice. She shivered, not from the cold, but the sensual tension that wound around her.

"Alone," she clarified.

"Shame," he said with a sigh. "But I'll take a good-night kiss instead as payment." He reached across the table, every action telegraphed and deliberate. His hands settled on her jaw and gently tugged her forward. "Because we both know, one day, we'll sort this mess out."

The kiss was light. Soft. His mouth barely touching hers, but every nerve inside her body quivered and jumped at the pleasure of the caress.

As he pulled away, his breath, warm and coffee scented, slid over sensitised skin. "We're good together. We always were. Give us a chance." Then he was up and gone while she sat there, lost in the web he'd woven around her.

CHAPTER 6

Tromping into the office the next morning, Thomas looked at Addie.

She raised an eyebrow. "Jack's meeting with the divisional heads in an hour," she informed him.

"Good. Can you track down these guys before then?" Thomas handed her a sheaf of paper, the names of people he knew and could count on scribbled across the page.

"Uh, maybe? I don't know them all."

"Mike'll know the rest. If you can get hold of him, he might track the others down. If they can be here by say, one this afternoon? We need to meet with Jack."

"Not one. Ultrasound," she said and rubbed her belly. "Make it two."

He sighed and agreed. It would cut their planning time severely, but he'd take what he could and be thankful.

Kelly entered the building and looked around. "Been a while since I've visited. Where's the rest of the staff?"

Addie shook her head. "Jack redeployed them. Tam's now at the shop with Sarah—"

"Oh yeah, I forgot that," Kelly said.

Addie ticked the staff who'd been still working in the office when she'd arrived on the island, on her hand. "Nadia and Stan are both working with the crew at the crematorium and taking an audit of who's here, who's died, and so on. The others have kids, so they're taking on extended child-minding duties and running the library on the mornings they're free."

"It's eerie to only have you two here all the time," Kelly said.

"It can get busy. When I need her, Tam comes in and covers for me. She'll take over when Junior," she said, and again rubbed her growing belly, "makes his appearance."

Kelly stilled and smiled at Addie, as if she felt joy, while Thomas watched on, trying to discern her real emotions from those she put on display. "It's a boy?"

Addie smiled. "I have no clue, but with the kicking, I better make sure there's lots of footballs in the house."

They all laughed, but Thomas was still wondering just how much of the emotion Kelly displayed was the 'act' she spoke of.

Jack came out of his office. "Did I miss a scheduled meeting?"

Thomas sighed. "No. But last night Jessica revealed more. Can we come in?"

"Sure." Jack moved aside to let them in. They settled at the large desk. "So, what more?"

Thomas looked at Kelly, willing her to explain. "She came into my room last night. Said there were two girls living with her in an abandoned house. They ran away when these zombies came to find them. She also said there'd been some older people, but the zombies killed them. She said they were 'picked off one-by-one' as if the zombies had planned it."

Jack stilled, his brow crinkled. "Planned?"

"They can swim. They're planning, and we think, based on what Jessica said, they have a crude form of communication. It doesn't bode well for us, Jack. Not at all."

"Fuck." He rose up, hands clenched. "If I knew who started this, I'd kill them, Thomas. I swear..."

"At the hospital, they had some ex-military types come through. I heard a whisper it was a government plot gone wrong. I don't know if that's true though," Addie said from the doorway, and they turned as a group to look at her.

"You never said anything," Jack groused.

"I didn't think of it until now. It was a rumour, and one no one ever got to the bottom of. I mean, if it's true…" Addie bit her lip, rubbed her belly, and lurched for the chair.

"Addie?"

"It's nothing. Just the body doing what it does to prepare itself for the baby." Her voice was soothing, but clearly it didn't settle Jack's nerves.

"I'm going to call Tam in. Cancel today's meeting."

"You don't need to, Jack. I'm perfectly fine. But we've got an appointment with Cherie later today. I'll go sit quietly and keep myself occupied if that settles your mind." Addie left the room.

Jack gave the appearance of a very worried man, and Thomas wondered once more how it would feel to be part of a new life growing. To have the responsibility for a family. He couldn't stop himself from looking at Kelly. Did she feel that way too?

"So, let's get down to business then. Tell me what you think." Jack's eyes narrowed.

"We go in. Find the girls, since they seem to be the magnet. If they're still there and alive, we rescue them, bring them back to the island. We'll need some families on standby, able to take them." Tom scratched his head.

"I got the impression from Jessica that they could be a bit problematic," offered Kelly. "They may need people used to dealing with difficult kids."

"Addie?" The woman popped her head around the door at Kelly's call. "Families with experience of kids with special needs? Mental health and so on. Do you know of anyone?"

"Possibly. I think one of the ladies who previously worked for Child Safety may know. I was chatting with her about the foster children currently on the island. She's of the opinion that they're all pretty settled, and we should make a formalised agreement that they be adopted by the families."

Jack nodded again. "None of this stuff would normally even come my way. Now, along with water and sewerage, we're dealing with educational issues, electrical problems at the hospital, and adoptions."

Thomas quirked an eyebrow. "I guess when you're in charge, that's the wages of sin and all that."

Jack harrumphed. "You want a team?"

"At least five others, along with Kelly and myself. Adequate munitions," he rattled off.

"There's a South Bay 925 CR in the marina. The guy who owned the boat died in the first virus wave, but his wife is still alive. If we could use that, we'd be able to move fast," Kelly explained. She named the widow and Jack wrote it down.

"I'll see what I can do. What else?"

"We need provisions, enough for a couple of days. Most importantly though, we need to move quickly. That does, however, leave Jessica," Kelly said.

"She could stay with us," Addie offered. "There's no issues with her behaviour, and she was great with the kids."

"We should be on the way in the morning if we can arrange it. Those kids are in danger, and if Jessica is right, their time could be up at any point. If we can save them, we should," Thomas said. "I've given Addie Mike's name and we'll get him to round up the others. We have a planning meeting this afternoon, and working together, we can be ready for an early morning departure."

"Okay. We chase them down, everyone goes. What happens if something goes wrong? 'Cause you know, this situation is unpredictable." Jack's question was fair in Thomas' estimation.

"We have flares on the boats. Two in quick succession means things are bad. One means we're on the way," Kelly offered. "Have someone on watch on the jetty where you guys got married. It's an excellent vantage point."

Finally, with Jack in agreement, Thomas and Kelly rose and headed for the front door. As they exited the building, Thomas reached out and grabbed Kelly's hand. "It's not too late to reconsider, Kel."

She turned and the brush of her long hair captured his attention for a brief second. "I won't change my mind, Tom. I'm in this with you."

"Together then?"

"Together."

CHAPTER 7

In Kelly's mind, night came quickly. The backpack she'd prepared for herself sat by the front door, along with the small bag they'd arranged for Jessica. Anything else she might need would be available to Addie anyway.

Thomas watched her, his eyes shadowed. "All ready?"

Kelly sighed. "I think so. A couple of changes of clothing. The medical kit is already stowed on the boat along with the provisions. The guys will arrive in the morning with the arms and munitions. I've got those life straws you found in the disposals place stashed in my bag too."

"You should get some sleep then, captain."

Kelly laughed, but it was a rasp to her hearing. *Can he tell how nervous I am? How much I almost fear this trip?* The refrain 'don't let them see' played on a continuous loop in her thoughts. It kept reinforcing the control she valued so highly.

What if you just let go?

Her gaze connected with Thomas'. "Kelly?"

"I'm..." The words stuck in her throat. She wanted and yearned, but to ask? Wasn't that releasing control? Would that leave her vulnerable?

"Tell me what you want, Kelly."

"I'm...scared. Thomas? What if this all goes wrong? What if something happens to you?"

He smiled, his lips stretching and turning upward slightly. "Same for you, Kelly. I don't want you to go, but you're right. You're the best we have. The best chance to find those girls and to learn about the zombies. I hate that. Inside me?" He thumped his chest. "There's a cold knot of fear. I'm not good with words, but you have to know, I'll do anything to protect you. To keep you alive, because without you, the world ceases."

Tears welled up, scorching her. Her hand reached and he took it and pulled her down until she was on his lap. A place she never thought to be ever again. His arms enfolded her, and the warmth of his body suffused her. He reached up and cupped her cheek as a burning tear slid down it.

***

"Don't cry, love. We'll get through this. So long as we're together, we can do anything, but promise me—" Thomas' voice turned husky. "—promise me you won't take any chances. If I say stop or down or drop, just do it. Please?"

"I will, but same goes. You're my offsider. You stay beside me on the boat, right? If anything happens to me, you have to know how to run the boat. I don't have time to train you properly, but you spent summers with us on the trawler and the personal craft. You know what you're doing."

"I will, but it won't come to that, okay?"

Kelly's body relaxed and he welcomed that, because it meant she was growing more comfortable with his advances. Ones he desperately wanted her to accept and reward in kind.

"Can I kiss you, Kelly?" he whispered.

For a second, she tensed, then released again. "Yes," she breathed.

Keep it light, Tom. Their lips slid against each other, and she sighed. It took every ounce of his iron will to refrain from deepening the caress. He yearned to taste her, but she wasn't ready yet, even though her body signalled otherwise. His body tightened and he groaned as he tugged away from her luscious lips.

"Thomas?" Her whisper clawed at him.

"No more. Not today. Not until you're ready. I promise you, I won't push beyond what you're comfortable with, no matter how hard that is. No matter how much I want you, I respect and care for you far too much to allow myself to cross that line."

"Don't respect me, Tom. Kiss me."

The tension beneath her grew, and his willpower wobbled. "Don't do this, Kelly. Not now. Neither of us is ready—"

She leaned in, her lips whispering along his jaw. "You feel ready to me."

"Damn it. I'm trying to respect you." Sweat beaded his upper lip.

Kelly sighed and pulled away. "I know. It's unfair of me. I'm sorry." She climbed from his lap, and he wanted to cry for her to return. "You want to do the right thing, and I'm pushing you. I appreciate the care you're taking with me. And I do want you. Really. I guess, though, it's easier to have the intimacy without the connection. It's all I've had since..." She blushed.

He considered her comment. "I've tried a few times, but they weren't you. I looked for women I thought might stack up against you. None of them did, because they weren't you."

Looking away, she wasn't quick enough to hide the silvery tear trails. "I never meant to hurt you, Tom."

Rising, Thomas moved in so he was just behind her. "I know, Kel. I know."

***

The boat cut through the water, and Kelly let the salty spray carried on the air wash away the last remnants of exhaustion. She hadn't slept well, and when Jack arrived this morning to drop off members of the team and to collect Jessica, it had been an effort to focus fully on the task. Now, behind the wheel of the boat, the crew onboard, she was waking up and feeling, if not better, then at least semi-human.

Thomas held out an insulated go cup. "Here. I thought a coffee might help."

Inside her chest, warmth flowed at the caring gesture. "Thanks." She took a grateful sip of the warm brew.

The mainland was rapidly approaching, and she turned the wheel of the boat, aiming for as close as possible to a hidden zone she'd noted on her last incursion. By agreement, she slowed the boat, so it chugged closer to the shoreline. Less noise means less to interest the zombies.

They left one crew member on the main boat and moved into the dinghy, and the tension now increased. Everyone looking and aware, because they'd all been told about the zombies she'd seen, and the tales Jessica had told. They didn't want to run into them unless absolutely necessary even though they were prepared.

She'd noted that the mangroves were lush and large, and she carefully angled the craft, not wanting the blades of the propellers to get stuck in them. She thanked providence that they weren't further north in the marshy mudflats hiding the root systems.

Satisfied with where they were hidden and aware they'd need to move silently but with speed, the others piled out, and she tugged on the oversized green tarpaulin they'd stashed and pulled it over the craft. They'd decided that though time was of the essence, it was essential to camouflage the vessel.

Once in the water they waded in the waist-high sludge to the banks and toward land. Looking down, Kelly grimaced at the way the brackish water left slimy streaks on the pants she'd chosen, but the guys were no better off, and for a moment, Kelly drank in the sight of the jeans Thomas wore, the way they plastered to his legs, betraying the muscles she remembered hidden beneath the heavy cotton material.

From the pocket on her backpack, Kelly withdrew the sheet of paper where Jessica had scrawled the instructions on how to reach the house. "We need to move quietly. Be always aware. We don't know where the zombies are nesting, just that they're hunting any humans."

The crew unsheathed the weapons. Some carried rifles, but she and Thomas both had smaller handguns; Kelly because she carried the first aid kit, and Thomas also carried a sword.

Rubbing bleary eyes, Kelly looked at Thomas. "A sword? What do you think you're going to do with that?"

He smiled. "If they get too close, a handgun will be less efficient with only six shots. This? Close quarters are where it's at its best. She's sharp." He flicked a piece of paper into the air. With a hiss, the sword cut through the air, slicing the paper into neat halves.

"Holy shit! When did you—?"

"A little something I learned not long after you cut me dead. I was angry and confused and needed an outlet. One of my instructors suggested it." He shrugged. "It made sense, and while I'm not competition quality, I can hold my own."

Now, Kelly was thankful for his forethought. As the sun rose, they moved in the formation they'd agreed upon, with Kelly in the centre and Thomas to her right.

They made their way through the brush, circling the edge of the city. Every sound magnified to her way of thinking, and she almost jumped when a hand landed on her shoulder. Turning, heart racing, she saw Thomas behind her.

"If we head up this street, then back four, we reach the crossways and shopping centre. We can cut through there, and it's about eight or nine streets along according to my map," Kelly said.

"Yeah," the sound was a wheeze from the man beside her.

"It's okay. The way looks clear right now. Take it as it comes. This is a marathon more than a race, love." Thomas' fingers caressed the exposed skin of her nape and she let it centre her.

"Okay."

Parting the greenery, they stepped out. Kelly's gaze darted back and forth, and she wondered if he'd felt like this on his mission many months ago when they'd found a container ship to fill and had saved Cherie and her family.

"Was it like this? Last time?" she asked.

He grunted and looked at her. "What?" The team halted around the two of them.

"When you saved Cherie and her family." Realising she'd stopped them, she stepped carefully forward, aware of the emptiness of the streets.

"Not quite. But we should save our breath and energy. We can talk later when we're in a safer location."

Feeling several shades of foolish, Kelly quietened and followed the others as they made their way along the eerily quiet road, littered with cars and refuse. Her hand on the butt of her pistol, sitting snug in the holster she'd attached once they'd climbed free from the murk, a heavy reminder of the danger that lay ahead.

The sun beat down on her, and sweat trickled down the back of her shirt, pooling at her spine with a prickle. Silence only punctuated by the occasional pant or word to still, wait, or continue ensured she stayed aware.

They rounded the buildings, and Thomas shoved her back, flattening himself against the building. "A nest ahead. I didn't count, but it looked like maybe ten or so. Our best bet is to wait here for a few minutes. See if they move on."

Plastered against the concrete, now hot from the sun, they waited in silence. Every couple of minutes, Thomas would carefully peer around the corner.

Time was a slow progression, sticky and interminable in her mind, but finally, with a whoosh of breath, Thomas whispered, "Looks clear. Mike on point. Move quickly but quietly. We need to make it down this block to the next without being seen."

They swarmed around the corner, each step sounding like a thud to her, though they were quieter, having worn gym shoes for this reason. The buildings around them were imposing, after spending so much time on the island with few buildings that were over four stories, and Kelly gulped.

"Tom! Incoming!" called Mike, and for a second, they stilled as a group in the time it took for a heart to beat, then legs pumped, propelling them forward as the low dirge of the zombie call echoed.

"Fuck," she muttered as Tom steered her around the corner.

"We need to get inside. Fine a defensible position," he growled, and three doors up, a building with the door wide open loomed. "In there." And they almost flew over the pavement.

Mike scuttled inside. "Clear," he called, and they piled in. Thomas turned and he and Mike slammed the door shut. The others grabbed whatever furniture they could find and barricaded the door.

The scent of decay filled the air, and Kelly swallowed the hard ball of bile which settled in her throat. "I can smell something, Tom."

He turned, sniffed. "I'll go look."

Kelly shook her head. "You're needed here. I'll go back." She indicated with her thumb to the rear of the store.

"Kel," he warned.

"I'll be careful, but you're needed here."

She scuttled forward, fearful of what she'd find but prepared for the worst. After all, she'd seen a lot in the last couple of years.

The small café had a back storage area, the heavy metal door barred along with the windows, and a large, cold room, still buzzing with power. The smell grew stronger as she headed for the kitchen zone.

That's when she saw it. The remains of a kangaroo, disembowelled and clearly partly eaten. The stink was putrid, ripe and sharp. Blood, dark and dry, smeared the floor, but long dried by the looks of it.

Kelly backed out, but not before she took the time to check here and there for anything else. Opening the door to the cold room, she peered inside and saw bottles of what she thought had once been milk with a grey-green tinge. Cream too, which had clearly gone off and fermented, before popping and coating the walls. "Could be worse." She refused to look at the meat at the back, fuzzy and overgrown with all kinds of bacterial growth.

Slamming the door behind her, she scuttled back to the front room where Thomas and the guys waited.

"Everything okay?" he muttered, dragging her close.

"Yeah. Wildlife in the kitchen, and I'd say the zombies have been in here judging by the state of the remains, but apart from that... If we clean it up, this is probably a good home base for us to work from." It wasn't too far from the boat, they could see clearly, and had access to cooking facilities and bathrooms.

"Maybe. So long as they aren't waiting around for us," Thomas added.

"There's a door to the rear and windows, so an alternative exit," Kelly explained.

When Thomas smiled, something inside her belly turned a somersault. "That's good thinking, love, and we can keep it in mind. Right now, our concern is how we can secure this location."

Thinking about the layout, Kelly wondered if there was a spot in the building in case the zombies got in. "The storeroom to the side might be an option, or the office?"

Thomas nodded, and she headed in the direction of those rooms. If they could find keys to the locks, they might be able to clean up the location sufficiently. Maybe set up some bedding? After all, if they were here for a couple of days, it would be worthwhile to have a setup prepared for their use.

Entering the storeroom, it was clear no one had stepped foot in here since the zombie mess started. Bottles of spring water sat upright in a corner, and on long, metal shelving were tinned, shelf-stable foods, but the room itself was clean, apart from dust.

She swiped her fingers over tins of fruits and vegetables. "Now they'll be welcome." Kelly smiled.

Cleaning products lay at the far end, blocked off with a large, plastic divider and a red sign screaming, 'Stop! Cleaning Products!' Thinking back to the carcass in the kitchen, she made note of the location of rubbish bags, mops, buckets, and floor cleaners. No matter how hard she looked though, there were no keys to be seen.

Pushing past the storeroom, she spied the door, emblazoned with 'office,' and shoved inside. Papers were strewn everywhere, and the safe door sat open. She ignored those and ratted through the drawers.

Nearly ready to give up, she found a set of keys in the last drawer in an unlocked metal cash tin. "Yes!" Flopping into the office chair, she took a moment to breathe and look around. "So much waste."

The truth was, with all the hurry and scurry of trying to survive, then focusing on a day-to-day existence, she hadn't really considered how things were on the mainland. It seemed remote and wild. Oh, she'd known things were bad, but suddenly, her own small issues didn't seem quite as insurmountable as before. Not when faced with the realities of the losses others had experienced.

"Kel?" Thomas had obviously followed her in, and she raised her head.

"Here." She thrust the keys at him.

"Everything okay?"

Kelly knew it wasn't perfect—the world wasn't perfect—and her perception of life hadn't changed in an instant, but finally, maybe she had a chance to make peace. The counsellor had told her, years ago, she had to make the first change. Embrace who she was, and ultimately make a choice to be happy after months of therapy.

"I've come to a conclusion, Thomas. I don't want to be angry forever. I deserve happiness and a chance to make something more of my life." Closing her eyes, Kelly considered her words. "I know now isn't the time, things are difficult and we're not really safe yet, but I think...when we get back to the island, it's time to talk, Thomas."

When she opened her eyes, there was an unfamiliar look of concern on his face. "Why?"

His question was fair, so she took a moment to consider how to answer it. "Because not everything is bad. I'd forgotten that, I guess. Seeing this," she said as she waved her hand to the room, "it reminds me that life goes on. Nothing is certain or easy, and things can and have changed in a heartbeat, but we've got lots to be thankful for."

The tension surrounding Thomas slowly melted from his frame. "Kelly, that makes me feel..." He shook his head. "Like I've told you in the past, I'm not great with words, but it makes me feel happy. Calm. But we need to get back out there and sort out our safe location."

She nudged his hand so the keys jangled. "I found them, so if they work, we give keys out to our group. Use this as a base. But first we need to clean up the kitchen."

He quirked an eyebrow.

"If things get ugly, we may need to hole up, like you said. There's tinned foods here, so we're good for a few days, and that means we don't have to rely on our provisions. They can be saved for next time, but the 'roo and the rot have to go."

"You think there'll be a next time?" He dropped into the chair on the other side of the desk.

"Until the zombies are gone, yes. While there's humans out there, in danger? We have a moral obligation to find and save them."

"What a woman," he muttered and rose. "Okay, we go check the keys."

"We get rid of the remains in the kitchen though, then we clean it up. And the stuff in the cold room." She followed his lead, climbing from the seat and walking out to the team.

They checked the doors and the keys worked. With one left, she cleared her throat. "There's an SUV somewhere around here." She called out the brand and more than one team member grinned.

"I drove one of them for a year or two, working as a parcel driver. They've got a few quirks, but if you know them..." Liam said.

"Shit car, but if it's still going, and has petrol, it should make looking for the kids and leading out the zombies easier," Mike offered.

"Don't know about that," muttered Dave, another one of the team. "After all, we have to put ourselves in danger before we find them. Me? I don't mind a fair fight, but from what Kelly has said, they aren't ordinary zombies."

Kelly shook her head. "No. They're bigger and meaner and faster. That any kids have eluded them for this long is no mean feat, but no one can afford to rest on their laurels, including us. We need to move fast, stay aware. Now, since Thomas already paired you guys up, I'm going to hand out keys. I've marked an 'f' for front on some and 'b' for back on others." Kelly handed them out to the pairs.

"You stick together. We can't afford to lose anyone from the team. We've got kids relying on us, and we need the intelligence to keep the island safe. We're the first line of defence. If we fail here, chances are everyone fails." Thomas' words sobered the group, and Kelly felt the responsibility now for her actions and the safety of all the islanders, including Jessica, the twins, and the new baby Addie was carrying as much as she guessed Thomas did.

"What do we...?" Mike asked.

"We clean the kitchen here first. Empty the cold room," Thomas answered.

"That doesn't make sense," called Liam.

Turning in a circle, Thomas looked at every member of the assembled team. "We turn this into a refuge. It's got food, water, and we can hole up in here. It's safer than anywhere else. But to stay well, we have to keep it clean. Stock it if we find foods, shelf-stable and long-life. We have a foothold in case, after this mission, we have to come back again."

"You think there's others over here?" Mike guessed.

Thomas nodded. "I do. If not here, then likely nearby. Most of you were with my team last time, when we grabbed the doctors and brought them back. You all know the situation. It's not pretty or nice. What we do saves lives. So, rather than blathering, let's get on."

He doled out jobs and they set to work, with Kelly on the mop while the men donned gloves and removed the offending and decaying remains. The cold room shelves were wiped clean, and she cleaned out the bloody streaks and pools. Dumping the water into the sluice drain, she sighed and wiped her brow.

"All good?" Thomas enquired.

"Yeah. I think we could almost use the kitchen now," she answered. "I've cleaned down the preparation area and found some bowls. We should eat before we head back out again."

"I'd like you to stay here, Kel." Thomas' words were like frozen lumps of ice were suddenly dumped in her belly.

"No."

Thomas' face was a mask. "Hear me out. I think we need to recon before we go out and look for the girls. It's a..." He reached up and clasped both hands on the top of his head. "It's a feeling. I just think we're going in blind and need some more info. I'm not even taking the whole team, just Mike and Dave. You stay here with Liam, Don, and Sam. We go out. Check the streets nearby. Two over each way. I just need to know if we're moving into a nest."

Her guts seized. "But you're in danger."

"Not so much. I'm fast, and so are the guys. We'll be armed, and we retreat back to here if we run into trouble." His words might make sense, but it didn't help that she was terrified if he went out that door he might not return.

"Tom." Her mouth dried. "Please, don't do this."

"I have to, Kel. I won't take risks, and I'll be back. Should only take a half hour or so." He dropped his arms. "I want to say—"

"No. You tell me when you get back." She grabbed him and kissed him hard. "You come back and tell me what you planned." Then she let him go.

His eyes were deep pools, and he searched her gaze before nodding and turning. The sound of his footsteps echoed until she couldn't hear them anymore.

CHAPTER 8

Thomas stepped onto the footpath and scanned the street. Car bodies, some clearly showing signs of conflict, littered them. They wouldn't look inside the vehicles. Today wasn't the time to deal with the remains of those long passed. They moved silently, taking care where they trod. Windows were smashed in some shop fronts, while others appeared intact apart from bloody smears.

Grass had begun spearing up through the asphalt road. Doesn't take long for nature to reclaim what was here before. They halted at the corner of the block and scanned the intersections.

"Straight ahead," he muttered, and they moved, keeping an even pace, but capable of speed should they need it. The traffic light blinked an intermittent yellow as they left it behind, and staying close to the buildings, they began a slow reconnaissance of the zone.

They knew there was a nest between their building and the water, but were there others in existence or had the majority of the zombies moved into the residential zones further out from the coastline?

A flash of colour at the end of the street had them sliding into a recessed doorway. "Kid," muttered Dave.

"Zombie?" asked Mike.

"Don't think so. Could be one of our targets," answered Thomas as they slid out.

The kid stood there, staring at them before pelting in their direction. Long strings of greasy, blonde hair slid down her shoulders, and the clothing she wore had clearly been appropriated from a high-end store. The sneakers on her feet were grimy, and Thomas' stomach ached at the knowledge this girl had been alone, trying to survive without someone to care for her.

"Hey! Who are you?" she called, and Thomas made a motion for her to be quiet as she finally stilled before him. "Nah. There's no zombs here."

"Are you Ellie or Jane?" He decided mincing his words under the circumstances wasn't worth the risk. When the girl stiffened, he knew she was one of the girls they were looking for.

"Why?"

"Jessica sent us to find you."

"She's alive? The zombs were moving pretty fast, and we had to split up. I thought for sure she was dead." She reached out a hand. "I'm Ellie. Jane is somewhere behind me."

Over Ellie's shoulder, Tom spied another girl, smaller and finer, with clean though short, black hair. Her clothes were an oversized t-shirt and leggings and well-worn running shoes.

She moved with reluctance up behind Ellie. "Whatcha want?" Her eyes narrowed. "Ain't got time for men." She spat on the ground, and Thomas could see past the tough exterior to a young girl who'd lived hard.

"I'm Thomas, and I guess you're Jane? We have a safe location, if you want to come with us. Kelly, another of our team, is making food. You'll be safe. Jessica sent her."

Jane—the tough girl—sneered. "She's dead. Didn't come back to our house."

"Because Kelly saved her. Took her to the island where she's being cared for."

The girl, tense and ready to fly, looked at Ellie. "If they can get us to safety, Jane, we should go."

"We're using an old café as a safe house," Thomas explained, naming it.

"I know it. Mum used to go there after she finished cleaning at Osprey." He knew the name of the exclusive clothing store, because more than one girlfriend had looked longingly at the ads in magazines. "She'd do an early morning then come home, and Dad would drop me at school," Ellie said.

An echo sounded, and the two girls stiffened.

"We need to move," said Thomas. "I'm going to carry you," he said to Jane, "and Mike'll grab Ellie."

They scooped up the girls and ran, because the reaction of the girls and his gut warned him that they didn't want to be out in the open when whatever was causing the noises arrived.

They pelted now, not really caring about staying quiet because getting to safety was the priority. At the block corner they stilled, hidden beyond the block of the building, and peered around.

The sight froze him. Three very large, very muscular zombies waited. They sniffed and turned in their direction.

"We need to get out of here now," growled Thomas, and once again the group of five moved, heading for the café. The door stood open, and Kelly was there. "Inside," he roared, and they ran through the door, slamming it shut. "Quick, get that counter," he panted, and the others shoved it before the door.

With fingers over his lips, he waited, tension turning his muscles to lead. They stood still, barely daring to breathe.

Sounds echoed from outside. He wanted to peer but wasn't game.

A roar echoed, and Kelly's gaze met his, her pupils dilated as her skin paled.

The girl in his arms shook like a leaf but remained silent. He guessed she'd been in this position before.

Time passed, and he wondered if it was safe. He started to slide the girl to the floor, but she clung like a limpet to him. He hugged her tight and waited some more.

Kelly moved, tiptoeing out of the room. Desperation clawed at him, but he stayed still because he didn't want to make any noise that might alert the creature outside. Dave followed her and came back long minutes later. "Kelly says come to the office," Dave whispered in his ear.

He nodded and moved with great care, the child still in his arms. Once in the storage area he breathed again. "What?"

"I decided to turn on the CCTV monitors. There's two there." She pointed to a zombie standing in the middle of the road. "Another up the road here." And she pointed to another view. "And a fourth on the other side. There's none at the back of the building."

He tensed and released. "Why none at the back if they're watching the front?" He rubbed his now aching head.

"Because they don't realise there's another way?" Kelly turned and looked at him. "It's clear they're working together and likely have some version of communication, but they don't have enough problem-solving abilities to realise there's more than one door. That's good for us."

"But they've changed since the initial zombies. They've evolved," said Mike, entering the office. "That's really bad news."

Everyone in the room nodded, and Thomas privately admitted that knowledge terrified him. "We need to gather data on them," Thomas said settled the girl on her feet, then turned in a circle and rubbed the back of his head as he thought.

"I think we've mostly seen enough," answered Kelly. "On a positive note, though, we found the car. I checked the fuel, and it's got plenty. It took two or three goes to turn it over—"

"You what?" He turned toward Kelly, and her smile died away.

"I went out and tried it. After we'd found the camera here. I had Sam come out with me, and Liam kept an eye on the camera. Don stayed by the door in case you came back."

Fury scorched. "You were meant to stay inside."

"No, Thomas. You wanted me safe, I made sure I was, but we had things that needed doing. We got them done. There's food on the stove, so we can eat in a few minutes. I checked the keys to the vehicle, and I moved it to just beyond the doors. Everything is ready for us to move quickly if we have to." Kelly rose from the seat as Mike ushered everyone else from the room.

"You should have followed my orders," Tomas growled and rubbed his chest where it ached.

"Bullshit. I'm a grown and independent woman." Her face tightened.

"You're part of my team, Kel. My responsibility." *My future, if you'd let me back in.* He kept those words to himself.

Her eyes glittered. "Well, you can fuck your team and yourself. I belong to me. Not to you, not to anyone." She made to storm past him, and Thomas grabbed her.

"You're not fucking blocking me out again. Not like last time."

"Get your hands off me, or I'll make you," she gritted out, her face hard and her eyes like frozen shards.

For a second, Thomas looked at her, stared long and hard, then released her. "Kel, I just want..."

Her bottom lip quivered, but she didn't back off. "I've lived with myself long enough to know I won't put myself in danger."

He opened his mouth, meaning to point out the risks she'd taken with the boat and picking up Jessica.

Kelly raised a hand. "I know what I did before. I know why I did it. Get me. I. Know." She balled her hands and inhaled. "I had a revelation earlier. It made me see what I've been doing for so long. Whether I like who and what I've been in the last few years doesn't really count. Not anymore. I realise I've been hiding. I know my triggers. Trust me, years of counselling does that for you." She laughed without any mirth. "But it also means, when you have one of those lightbulb moments, you examine it. Consider it." She shook her head and glanced away for a second before spearing him with a hard glare. "I have no intention of placing myself into a position I can't survive. I found the car because it was nearby, but I didn't take any chances. I parked it after checking the fuel because it occurred to me, if we have to move quickly, we need a way. This gives us capacity."

Every word she spoke hammered into his brain. *Did I react badly because she's a woman? Or because I care so much about her?* Honesty forced him to accept the latter. "I'm sorry, Kel. I should have let you tell me without jumping down your throat."

Kelly cocked her head. "Yes, you should have. I understand why. I may struggle with it from time to time, but I do understand. I'm trying hard to give us options. You're trying to keep us safe. They are compatible even if you don't like what I've done."

"Guys? We've got food out here," Mike called.

"We should go eat. This is a conversation for later. Once we're home," Thomas added.

***

Following him to the kitchen, Kelly worked hard to control her emotions. Everything she'd said was honest, but his problem with her working to keep them safe? That was completely different. If they did get a second chance, would he be a 'keep the little woman safe' proposition? Or would he accept she could think and execute a plan too? As youngsters they'd never had the chance to find out. Never had the need.

She shoved the thought away as she accepted a bowl of steaming soup. Her mouth watered as the lumps of chicken—dried and brought with them from the island—rose to the surface. The dried buns they'd carried an accompaniment.

The girls tucked in, clearly ravenous. The adults watched and refilled their empty bowls without a word. The food was consumed in silence, then they all settled back on the chairs to plan the next stage.

"We found meat in the freezer," Sam said, as if looking to soothe the high emotions still echoing in the room.

"Good. I think the plan to keep this as a base is sound." Thomas nodded. "Mike, what's your thoughts on those zombies?"

"They're bigger and certainly far more dangerous than any we've come across before. Girls, Jessica said they can swim."

Jane, the obviously younger girl, nodded. "I saw them. Not sure how far they can go, but they're getting faster too. You know, like how one year you're slow but the next you get a bit faster?"

That news boded badly for them all. It was as if their evolution was speeding up, and when Kelly glanced up, she saw the same knowledge in the eyes of every adult at the table.

"We're not going to be able to keep them out forever," whispered Kelly, and now her eyes burned with tears.

"We'll find a way, Kel. It won't be easy, but we'll find a way."

***

By unspoken agreement, the crew cleared and cleaned, while Thomas and Kelly retreated to the office to make their plans for the next day. Peering at the monitor, they noted the zombies had moved away from the door.

"We're going to have to be quick getting back to the boat," she said. "It's going to take time to uncover it and get out of the swamp."

"I have an idea," he countered.

Kelly glanced at Tom.

He grimaced. "I'm going to drop you, Sam, and Liam at the swamp with the kids. The rest of us are going to head for the jetty. You need what, ten or fifteen minutes tops to get into the water?"

"I may be able to do it faster," she muttered, but his words resonated. With fifteen minutes she'd have everyone ready and be just about there. So long as nothing went wrong.

"Work on fifteen. We drop you, then we take off. We draw them away. Lead them through the streets." He tugged out a map he'd found on the brochure display. "We go this way. Keep them running. At the twelve-minute mark, we head back this way—" He drew a slashing line. "—heading for the jetty. We pull up and pile out. You're there and off we go."

"There's lots of places where they could cut you off. Here and here." She pointed, and he grunted.

"Then we go this way." His fingers traced a different direction. "You need time. We need space."

Glancing at his face, Kelly sighed. "I'd feel better if you didn't have to do that."

He cupped her cheek, sliding a thumb over it. "I'd like that too. But we need to outrun them, and we know they're fast. It's not a luxury that we have."

"No," she whispered. "I know."

Jane entered the room. "I know where their nest is. Take me with you and I'll show you."

Tom's head shot up before he shook it. "Tell me where, because I'm not—"

"Jeez Louise! I know I'm a kid, but I know more about them than you do, right?" the girl bellowed. "I know about their human guides—"

"What?" Shock ricocheted through Kelly at Jane's words. "Humans working with them?" How...? That couldn't possibly be right, could it?

"Not so much working with them. The humans have the zombs in a caged area." Jane spat the words out. "They have these sticks and prod them. Makes them angrier. Jessica didn't know. She was soft like Ellie, but I know. I watched them. Lots of times." The light in her eyes was furious, and unease spread through Kelly.

"Fuck," muttered Thomas. "Okay, I'm not taking you, but draw me an 'X' so I know where to look."

The girl smiled. "The humans have cars and trucks," she said as she scratched out a wobbly symbol.

Kelly and Thomas' gazes collided. "Fuck me," he growled.

She slid a hand over Thomas' chest and imperceptibly shook her head. "We need to know, but maybe there's another way."

"What?"

"Jane, is there somewhere he can see from? Safely? A building top?"

The girl nodded. "The Osprey building. It's the tallest in town. The zombs and humans don't go there. I used to watch from there. I've got some...you know," she said as she pantomimed eyeglasses with her hands.

"Binoculars?" clarified Kelly.

"Yeah," muttered Jane.

Kelly filed that away for reference. There had to be a reason why she had them, but she wouldn't ask. Not now. "We get up there, take a look. Get as much info as we can, then we make our run."

He didn't like that, she could tell by the way his body hardened beneath her touch, but she needed him to calm down, just a little. The girl was used to being in charge, and they needed to handle her very carefully. They also needed to make plans for everyone's safety.

Sending Jane out to get Mike, she took a moment. "You need to calm down, Tom. That girl? She's had a rough time, and it's hard to remember she's not an adult, but that's something we have to remember, because anything else is bad for all of us."

He jerked away. "I know. But I feel like I'm fighting shadows with a hand tied behind my back."

She nodded, because she too felt that.

By the time Mike entered the room, they had a rudimentary plan ready to share.

"You're sure about this?" Mike queried at the end.

"It's all we've got right now," Tom explained.

"Then we split into two groups. Kel, me, and you go to the Osprey. The rest stay here and get ready to move on our signal."

"Liam should drive. He knows that model well," Kelly suggested, thinking back on his words when they'd found the keys.

"Makes sense." Thomas looked at the doorway to Jane, who'd followed them. "You stay here with the team. Do what they say."

Jane shrugged. "If you want."

They hustled out of the room and grabbed weapons, checked the safeties as a matter of course. Thomas checked the flares in his backpack, then the three of them slid through the now unlocked door and out onto the street.

Every step was taken quickly as they arrowed across the road, having worked out the best route. Two blocks along they turned right. Thomas stopped them, and Kelly took a moment to slow her heartrate.

"Clear," he murmured, and off they went again, jogging toward the large, grey tower which rose above the other buildings.

Fingers on lips, they slid to a stop at the door which was gaping open. She could see remains littered, and the horrific sight reminded her that they too could end up like that if they didn't take care. They made it to the steps and kept going. There was no way they intended to be caught in an elevator.

The steps were steep; her legs ached, but there was no time to rub them or stop. They moved ever upward, and at the top Thomas reached out, turned the handle, and opened the door.

The rooftop was open to the elements. No rooftop garden or eatery, and she thanked everything for that. Large air conditioning vents sat proud, and she realised they were silent. In one corner she spied a mound of pillows, and they advanced, crouching low to remain out of sight.

As she glanced down, she saw the compound Jane spoke of. The large wire netting, the twin towers at the front, and jury-rigged metal walkways above leading to a squat, concrete building.

A mass of zombies meandered around, several gazing out beyond the confines of the fencing. In the distance came the whine of two trucks. The four zombies who'd chased them moving ahead, growling and moaning.

A stick poked out and jabbed the largest.

It turned, grabbed the stick, and as one, the four zombies stopped, gripped the front of the car, and pushed it. A whine split the air.

"Oh Jesus," muttered Kelly.

The other car closed the distance and one of the four zombies roared.

In the compound a louder echo started.

"They're communicating," breathed Mike. "Fighting back. See them pulling on the fence?" And they were.

As if Thomas had seen enough, he pulled them both back. "We have to move now. Get out of here."

They pelted across the roof and down the stairs, the sound of zombie discontent growing louder.

Gunshots filled the air as Thomas tugged her from the shop. "Run, Kel. We gotta get out of here."

Her lungs burned, legs churning as they arrowed in the direction of the café. Not that it was a long-term refuge, but if they could make it out the back before the zombies found them…

They dashed through the front door with chests heaving from exertion. "Lock it," she shrilled and then pushed the kids in the direction of the back of the cafe. "Through the back door and into the car. Liam, we gotta go. Leave everything behind."

Terror telegraphed, and the entire team moved. Once they were piling into the car, she turned and locked the door before sprinting and climbing in beside Thomas.

He clutched her hand, and she didn't look back. Didn't dare. Moments passed with only the whine of the engine filling the air.

Liam drove fast, and she was sure he was taking the corners on two wheels. Soon they were at the edge of the marshy underbrush. She, the men that would come with her, and the children climbed out.

For a second, her gaze clashed with Thomas'. "Be safe," she croaked, then the car shot forward, and she was ushering them in the direction of the boat.

Trudging through the thick muck, Kelly was just pleased the girls didn't complain too much, other than, "Eww, this is gross."

At the boat, she motioned the girls to be quiet, and the assembled team members tugged the cover off the boat.

"Sweet," breathed Ellie, and Kelly could hardly supress a smile.

Once everyone who needed to be aboard was secured in the dinghy, the guys pushed and the small craft came free of the sucking mud. They climbed aboard and she started the engine, the throttle revving as she backed it out and headed for the jetty.

"How long?" she called to Dave.

"Twelve minutes," was his reply, and she gulped. It would be close run to make the fifteen they'd agreed upon.

CHAPTER 9

The jetty lay in front of the vehicle, and they swung in, the car sliding. Liam cut the engine, and they climbed out. The zombies they'd caught sight of weren't far behind them as Thomas scanned the horizon.

"Come on, Kelly," he muttered as they jogged to the end of the jetty.

A roar sounded and they looked up. The zombies were fast approaching as the whine of an engine split the air. The boat sped toward them, water spraying up behind it, as Kelly cut through the water. They waited, one eye on the zombies and another on the craft.

It swung, the spray soaking them. "Get ready," he called to the others as the zombies approached the jetty. As the craft came alongside, they slid in.

"Hold on," screamed Kelly, and they arrowed forward, the g-force nearly tumbling them from the boat as the zombies reached the end of the jetty.

Several jumped in the water and started moving arms and legs in an approximation of swimming. Some distance out, Kelly cut the throttle, and Thomas climbed across the seats and in beside her.

The team watched, horrified to see the development. "I've seen enough. Let's get out of here," he growled, and Kelly once more set the throttle to open, and they headed for the much larger craft she'd moored nearby.

Once aboard the fishing vessel, she settled the children in the cabin then started the engines. They made reasonable time, not as fast as their earlier trip, but Kelly explained with the extra bodies she wanted to conserve their fuel. Several hours passed before they reached the island.

Carefully motoring into the main jetty, they scanned the island.

"Is that where Jessica is?" asked Ellie.

"Yeah," Thomas answered.

"Nice. I like this boat," Ellie said and giggled.

"Shut up, idiot," Jane snapped at her.

Kelly and Thomas glanced back at the girl. He understood she had issues with authority that would need to be addressed, but right now? All he felt was a sense of relief that they'd survived. Not that he wasn't aware that bigger and worse dangers were coming for them, but right here and now, with Kelly beside him, he could relax.

***

Kelly stretched, her hand on the small of her back, trying to be surreptitious. Hours of worry, the wild running around, and the pressure of staying quiet had taken their toll. Not to mention the two-day mission had taxed her.

"You alright, Kel?" Thomas' query surprised her.

"Yeah. Just a long day, you know." She glanced at the two girls swinging their legs on the end of the jetty.

A car drew up, and Jack, Jessica, and Addie climbed out. Jessica helped Jack with Leanne and Fiona, while Addie waddled her way along the wooden planks, her face strained.

"Hey, Addie. Is everything okay?" Kelly called.

As she stepped forward, Addie doubled over, hand on her belly. "Argh!" A trickle of pinkish fluid coated the inside leg of her pants.

"Addie?" Jack bellowed.

"We need the ambulance!" called Thomas.

The two girls raced up to Kelly. "Go help Jessica with the babies," she muttered and looked about for somewhere to settle Addie.

"Thomas, go get Roz. We're going to need her now!" She kept her voice controlled but firm, and Thomas rushed away to do her bidding.

"Kelly? My baby. It's too soon," sobbed Addie.

"We'll do everything we can, Addie. Jack, lift her and we'll go to the chair over there." She pointed to a bench at the end of the walkway beside the jetty. "Do you have any blankets?"

Jack nodded in the act of lifting Addie with a grunt and staggered with her in his arms. "In the boot."

Kelly looked up, but Thomas had taken the vehicle. She noted the taillights in the distance and sighed, then shrugged off her backpack. There was a space blanket in the medical kit, and this was an emergency.

"Keep her calm, Jack," she said as he settled Addie on the bench. Unzipping the bag, Kelly's hands shook as she hunted for the kit she'd stashed in the bottom. Gripping the hard, moulded plastic, she reefed it out, unclipped the box, and found the item she required. "Do you have any names chosen yet?"

Addie's eyes met hers. "No, we thought we'd have more time. Besides, we decided to wait and see if it's a boy or girl before picking the name that best suited. I had a check-up the day before yesterday, and everything was good."

"You looked uncomfortable coming up the jetty."

"I've had twinges yesterday and today. I thought they were Braxton Hicks, so I ignored them, because I had heaps with the twins." Addie moaned her way through the words, and Kelly glanced at Jack, who was clearly terrified.

"Kel...?"

She shook her head. "Thomas has gone for the ambulance. They won't be long. Now we just need you to calm down. Breathe nice and deep and concentrate on something relaxing."

Kelly wasn't sure this was going to do the trick, but all the movies she'd watched with birthing women had them controlling their breathing. That has to help, right? She might be feeling more than just slightly panicked, but she'd hold her shit together even if it killed her.

"Jack, lie her down on the bench, with her head on your lap. She'll be more comfortable that way."

He moved to accommodate Addie, and Kelly readjusted the blanket. She didn't dare look to the children standing by. Right now, her focus was Addie.

Jack whispered in Addie's ears as she laid there, her face screwed up as each pain came and went.

"Hurry up, Thomas," Kelly muttered under her breath, fingers clenched as she scanned the road.

A wail sounded in the distance, coming closer, and she breathed a sigh of relief. Trained medical assistance wasn't far away. When the ambulance pulled up alongside the bench, Kelly almost cried with relief.

A slim woman slid from the cab, her hair a short, silvery blonde. "What do we have here?" Her voice was slow and reassuring, but her eyes were keen, as if picking out every fact she could.

"Addie's thirty-five weeks," Jack answered.

"She was joining us on the jetty, when she started, I don't know, leaking? Bleeding?"

"Addie's your name?" She crouched beside Addie and took her hand. "I'm Roz, and I'm going to take good care of you. I need to look under the blanket, is that okay?"

Addie nodded and Roz smiled.

"I've had twinges since yesterday." Addie groaned. "Today they were more intense." She gasped and clutched Jack's hand. "Now it's just one long pain with..." She squeezed her eyes shut. "...with peaks." When she reopened them, there were tears leaking down Addie's cheeks.

"Good girl." Rising, Roz moved along and lifted the blanket out of the way. "I need to take off your pants to have a look." She reached into her pockets and removed a pair of gloves. They slapped as she put them on. "Kelly can help me. Jack, you keep doing what you're doing there."

Kelly lifted the blanket while Roz manoeuvred into position, carefully grasping the layers of clothing and peeling them away.

Thomas arrived and Roz shook her head to keep him back. "Look after the kids. Take them down to the shop or something," she instructed. "Addie doesn't need an audience."

Glancing over the space blanket at Addie, Kelly smiled. "I've known Roz most of my life. She'll look after you both," she assured her, while determinedly ignoring whatever it was Roz did.

"Okay, drop the blanket down now," the paramedic instructed. "I'm going to collect the gurney, and once we've got you in the ambulance, I'm going to call Cherie to help me. Kelly, you're my assistant here. Alright?"

Addie groaned through another contraction and Kelly's guts churned. "Will—"

"Not now, Kelly. Let's get the gurney." Roz moved with controlled grace, and Kelly followed her to the ambulance. "This is a two-person job." Opening the back of the ambulance, Kelly goggled at the mini-consulting room within.

"I've never seen inside an ambulance," she muttered.

"Most people haven't." Roz gripped the end of the gurney and tugged it. When it was almost out, she stopped. "There's a latch on the side, then pull down the base."

Kelly followed her instructions, and Roz indicated she should pull the bed a little further out.

"The safety latch," she said then pulled a folded blanket from the seat. Together they moved the wheeled bed to beside Addie. "Jack, lift her on and we'll get her in the ambulance."

Working together, but not rushing or jarring, they moved Addie onto the bed and covered her with a blanket then wheeled her over to the vehicle.

Once settled in the ambulance, Roz set the scene. "Jack, you sit here at the head end, you're going to support Addie. Kelly, you're here, okay? I'm going to call Cherie and get her over here, rather than move Addie at this point." She shoved a pair of latex gloves in Kelly's direction. "And put those on."

Before she climbed from the ambulance, Roz conducted another inspection, lifting Addie's legs up and apart. "Well, Junior is in a hurry." She smiled at Addie, and Kelly could tell it was to settle her nerves. Then she turned to Kelly. "If she needs to push, you call. If the baby crowns, you yell."

Kelly squirmed. "But..." She knew what crowning was, but this wasn't a position she'd ever expected to be in. After all, it wasn't like she'd seen another woman's vagina up close and personal before.

Roz gripped her arm. "She's in labour, and it's moving fast. I can't stop it because of the speed. I need you to pay attention, Kelly, because we're all counting on you."

Kelly gulped and nodded, feeling a trickle of sweat down her spine. Roz's words reinforced just how dire the situation was.

Addie moaned and arched.

"It's okay, Addie. We'll all see you right," Roz soothed. With a single last look at Kelly, Roz slid out the door of the ambulance.

"Jack? I'm sorry," groaned Addie as tears slid down her face.

Jack's face mirrored Addie's for the pallor. "It's not your fault, love."

"I... Oh no! I need to push!" Addie screamed, and Kelly was terrified.

What if the baby comes shooting out quickly or something goes wrong? I know nothing about giving birth! "Roz!" Kelly called, and the door opened. "She needs to push."

Roz clambered back inside and looked for a cupboard, tugging the bag from the container inside. "Okay, love. Let's do this together. I need to get you comfortable." Roz raised the back of the stretcher. "We're a bit short on space, but that should help. Now, I know this isn't your first time, but each is different. You tell me if something feels wrong, okay?"

Addie nodded.

Roz settled on her haunches between Addie's legs. "I can see the head."

Kelly couldn't look away. Slowly, as Addie huffed and grunted, the head emerged.

"Doing good," coached Roz as she slid her hands under the baby's neck. "Another push when you're ready, love."

Slowly, inch by inch, the baby emerged, before slithering into Roz's waiting hands. It wailed as Roz called to Kelly to grab the blanket.

"Addie, undo your shirt and I'll pop your baby girl on your chest," Roz said.

Addie was crying but complied, and with the baby safely nestled in, Roz draped the blanket over both, as the baby cried.

Kelly couldn't help the tears flowing down her cheeks. "Will the baby...?"

"It's looking really good. A nice size and crying up a storm," Roz soothed before stripping off her gloves and opening the door. "Lose your gloves in here." She pointed to a large waste receptacle in the corner. "And Kelly? You did good."

As Kelly climbed from the ambulance, it was into a sunset of orange and violet hues and to see a car rushing toward them. Cherie jumped from the passenger side and hurried over. "I'm here!" she called and climbed inside. The door shut behind her, and Kelly sighed with relief.

CHAPTER 10

Before the ambulance took Addie to the hospital, Jack climbed out. "Can you take the kids home and stay at our place tonight? Addie made some food for the girls, and it's in the fridge," he told Thomas.

"Sure." It wasn't quite what Thomas had in mind, but given the circumstances... He shrugged. Life in the middle of a zombie apocalypse goes on. For now, anyway, his cynical brain added.

"Come on. Let's grab clothes for the girls," Thomas said as he ushered the three girls, two toddlers, and Kelly. "Then we'll head back to Jack and Addie's."

Kelly appeared shocked, and speechless too. She simply complied, and together, they grabbed underwear, shoes, and clothing for the girls, loading it into the car. He settled Fiona and Leanne into their seats with the help of Jessica and Kelly.

"I'll walk with the girls. It's not far." Kelly still appeared pale, and Thomas wanted to argue, but the knowledge of what kind of mischief the girls could get into unchecked had him swallowing his words.

Climbing into the car, he drove slowly. As Kelly said, Jack's house wasn't far from the jetty, so even as he was climbing from the vehicle the four wandered into the yard.

Silently, Kelly reached out and unhooked Leanne, then swung her up into her arms. "I think she needs changing," she muttered, and he couldn't miss the unmistakable whiff as she handed over the toddler. "I need to shower and change before I do anything else."

Cursing his bad luck, he instructed the girls to assist him. Jessica already knew the process. She merely wrinkled her nose, unlike the other two who complained loudly.

"Ewe, gross!" Jane whined.

"I think I'm going to be sick," added Ellie, and she pinched her nose.

In the background, he heard the whoosh of water and knew Kelly was cleaning herself up. She'd closed herself away again, and he hated that knowledge.

Finishing up with the changing of both babies, he offered one to each Jane and Ellie and ushered them all into the kitchen. Once the babies were installed in highchairs, he had the girls wash their hands and he set about making a rudimentary meal for them all, while heating the baby food Addie had prepared earlier.

The eggs were cooked, the toast buttered and laid on plates as Kelly came into the kitchen. "Eggs on toast, huh?"

He shrugged. "Easy, and there are plenty of bread and eggs, so we're making the best of it."

Jane was spooning food into Leanne's mouth like a pro, and he wondered about the girl's background. Jessica was urging Fiona to feed herself, a messy prospect as more slopped on the tray than in the baby's mouth, but given the gurgling laughter, Thomas didn't worry.

"You've done that before?" Kelly asked Jane.

The girl's eyes flashed with pain. "Before this mess I had three little sisters. They got sick straight away and died."

Kelly reached out and touched the girl's hand. Jane flinched but Kelly hung on. "We all lost people, Jane. It's okay to be sad and angry."

"Who did you lose?" she growled, and Kelly's lips turned down.

"Most of my friends. The people who were there for me when my life was rough," she whispered. "My mum died just before the plague, and I lost my dad a week ago."

Thomas felt a shaft of pain through his heart. She'd lost everyone, and he felt like a poor substitute. "Kel..."

She shook her head and he quieted, understanding she needed time to come to settle after today's efforts.

The blare of the walkie-talkie caught his attention, and he shot out of his chair. "Thomas here."

"It's Jack. Addie and the baby are doing well. Can you come get me soon?"

The news echoed in his mind. Doing well. "When will Addie be home?"

"In a couple of days. She's got some stitches, but the baby is super healthy, and they will likely discharge them both at the same time." Jack sounded both relieved and proud, and Thomas, while still not understanding all the whys and hows, could understand the pleasure in Jack's voice.

"We're just eating, then I'll come get you."

The meal passed in near silence, apart from the toddlers' antics and chortles, and everyone mucked in to clean up.

"Right, I'm heading up to the hospital to get Jack. Need anything?" he murmured to Kelly.

She shook her head. "No. I'll get the bedding settled for the girls here in the lounge, and we can take the fold-out bed in here. Keep an eye on them."

If he didn't know better, he might have guessed she was disappointed that they wouldn't get to talk as freely as they'd both wanted. He shrugged, and gathering up the keys, he headed down the stairs to the car.

Jack was waiting under the portico when he arrived and stopped the engine. Thomas climbed out, offering Jack the driver's seat. Wordlessly, Jack accepted the keys Tom handed him.

As they both got in, Jack sighed. "The baby... She's a beauty, and Addie's going to be fine." But he sat there, gripping the wheel. Staring into the distance. Moments, long and heavy, drew out.

"Jack?"

"It's just... She was in so much pain, and I thought I was going to lose her, Tom. I can't..." Jack shook his head. "I can't do that. She's my everything." The words croaked out, as if squeezed under pressure.

"We can't live our lives focussing on the what ifs," Thomas offered. "We have to grab the opportunities we have with both hands. Make the best of what we have."

Jack nodded silently and turned the key. The engine fired up, and they drove slowly back to the house.

"Have you thought of a name yet?" Thomas asked.

"Yeah. Roslyn Kelly, after the two women who brought her safely into the world." He turned to Thomas. "Kelly's pretty fucking special, and this time, you have to make her see that."

Thomas sighed and looked through the windscreen. "I'm trying, but she's prickly. There's... Stuff happened." He refused to share the details. They weren't his to give, and only if she gave permission would he share.

"I know she went to counselling. She was different after you two broke up. Like a part of her died. Lately though, I'm seeing a spark of the old Kelly. The same, but different."

Laughing, Tom nodded. "Yeah. It's as if a new Kelly has come out of the cocoon." The laughter died away. He stilled, frowned. "I love her, Jack."

"I know. Hell, she knows it too. But your father... He did a job on her. I was there one time when he contacted her. Before the trial. It..." Jack turned into the driveway. "It nearly broke her. After that, she stopped answering unknown numbers ringing her cell, barely went anywhere. Her dad got rid of the television then. Didn't want her watching the trial updates on the news. He'd listen to the news on the radio out of her earshot. Took her to counselling. I remembered one day he threatened to shoot the fucker if he came anywhere near her again. When he returned to the island, those who knew the truth protected Kelly anyway they could."

Gutted, Thomas leaned back into the seat and gulped down air, hoping to soothe the nausea that rose. "I didn't know."

"She refused to let us tell you. Your mother understood Kelly's trauma, but your father kept her on a tight leash. We tried to help her too, but your mother refused to leave him."

"If that sonovabitch was still alive, I'd kill the fucker," Thomas growled, fury infusing his words.

"He's not. Something everyone I know is thankful for, Tom. He's not worth the effort."

"He still haunts Kelly."

Jack nodded. "Yeah, I know. If we can help—"

"We need time and privacy to talk. Without the kids."

"It's the weekend, Tom. Not sure how…"

"You had a list of foster carers, I thought," Thomas reminded his best friend.

"Yeah. If that's what you think is best." But there was a question behind Jack's words.

"Jessica's okay, but the other two need more than we can give. We also need to report what we saw. It's bad, Jack. Really bad."

"Tomorrow will be soon enough. Let's get inside and give Kelly a break."

CHAPTER 11

Waking up was like ascending through layers of clouds. The room was quiet, and opening her eyes in Jack and Addie's lounge, Kelly saw the bedding in neatly folded piles on the floor.

"Thomas?" she groaned.

Silence greeted the words, and she crawled from the cocoon of the blankets. Padding to the bathroom, she noted the house remained silent. Where is everyone? After quickly using the facilities, she exited the room and wandered down the hallway.

Checking the kitchen, she discovered a bowl of cereal and a bottle of milk on the table. The condensation ring told her she'd been abandoned at some point earlier. Making her way out to the deck, she squinted, and there, over the road, were Jack, Tom, and the five kids. The three older ones were rolling balls along the sandy ground to the toddlers.

As if he could feel her gaze, Thomas looked up and waved, before standing, brushing himself off, and heading toward her. Suddenly conscious of how dishevelled she must appear, Kelly ran her fingers through the strands of hair.

Thomas met her at the top of the stairs. "Have you eaten?"

She shook her head.

"Come on then, I'll make us both a coffee while you eat."

"What about the others?" She pointed to Jack and the kids.

"We ate earlier while you snored."

"I don't snore," she answered, somewhat miffed by his choice of words.

"Delightfully soft, whiffle snores. Like a kitten or a puppy." He laughed, heading for the kitchen, and Kelly followed him. "Now sit down and eat. We need to talk," he said as he prepared the hot water. "About the girls. I don't have the skills or the patience for Jane and Ellie."

The dish and cereals were laid out, so she dumped some into a bowl and added milk. Lifted the spoon then grimaced. "I don't think either of us does," she said. "But what...?"

"I spoke with Jack beforehand, as you know, and he's gathered a list of names. There's a woman who was with Child Services, and she's going to swing by later and evaluate the kids. Jack and Hayley have been sifting through the list of possible carers, and they think they may have a plan to keep Jane and Ellie together. And Jessica too, if you and she are amenable to that plan."

Considering Thomas' words, Kelly nodded. "Jessica's great, but I don't think I'm cut out to parent a teenager on my own."

"And we're going to be busy, Kelly. Now that we know the truth, we need to train others. You need to show others how to run boats and me to use the armaments. We need to prepare, because they know how we got to the mainland. It's just a matter of time."

Kelly winced. "I don't want her to think I'm abandoning her."

"I get that. But you're better as a kind of cool older sister," he teased and poured the water into the cups he'd laid out and added coffee grounds to.

"Cool older sister, huh?"

He carried the cups to the table and settled opposite Kelly. "Yeah, something like that. Besides all that, we need to sort out the 'us' situation too."

"Us situation," Kelly parroted.

He nodded. "I'm not letting you go. Not again. Yesterday I would have died for you. I still would. Watching you with Addie, the way you calmed her and seeing you take charge? The strong woman you've become is precious to me, and I've been a fool to wait this long."

"To be fair, it wasn't just me. But we need to focus on—"

"Living our lives. Taking the opportunities. We don't know how long we have. The plague showed us that. I don't want to waste any more time. I need you. I know you need me."

"I..." She gulped. "I do. But I'm scared, Tom. Last time it hurt when things went wrong."

"It will always hurt when things go wrong, love. But we can't ignore a chance because we might get hurt, otherwise we'll both be alone for the rest of our lives."

She opened her mouth, then closed it. Looking like a gasping goldfish isn't going to endear you to him.

"Now, this afternoon we have Child Services here, meeting with the girls. Jack's going to talk to them about it once you've eaten, leaving us to be a kind of back-up in case they take it into their head to cut a runner. Then tomorrow morning, we're convening here for a council of war with the divisional leaders, letting them know what we found. Thomas and I agree a public meeting is in order, so we're rounding up the buses to bring everyone to the auditorium on Monday evening."

"Sounds like you were both doing a bit of planning while I slept."

"Well, the twins woke early, and I made coffees while he changed them and gave each of them a bottle. Then Jane, Ellie, and Jessica woke up and were hungry, so we ate and decided to take them to the park and let you rest a little longer."

"I'm not a weakling," she grouched, finishing her cereal and looking at the coffee. "You should have woken me."

"Why? Nothing can happen until this afternoon. Jack's waiting for our signal and will bring the kids back, then he'll talk to them. Seriously, you sleeping a bit longer didn't affect any plans at all."

"Has he spoken to Addie? How's the baby? Does she even have a name?"

"Yes, he spoke with Addie earlier. The baby is doing great and doesn't appear to need any intervention. And yes, she has a name. Roslyn Kelly."

The oxygen was sucked from her lungs as he announced the name. "Roslyn Kelly?"

"Named in honour of Roz who delivered her and for you. I'm so proud of you, Kelly."

Her senses jumbled and tears threatened. "Why me? I didn't do—"

"You kept everyone calm, took charge until the cavalry arrived, then assisted. I reckon you've earned the honour, love."

***

Thomas waited by the door, having agreed with both Jack and Kelly that they didn't need any of the girls to disappear before Hayley, the Child Services officer, arrived. Jessica had been sullen, though she agreed that being reunited with Jane and Ellie was the best option.

"It's not that I don't want you, Jessica, but there's a lot about to happen. I need you safe," Kelly explained.

"But I'll be good, Kelly. I'll do everything you say." Jessica looked crushed, and Kelly grabbed the youngster's hand.

"I need to do my job, and I need you to help me. The way you do that is by going with Hayley. I trust her, and she'll keep the three of you together."

"But we could stay with you."

Kelly inhaled. "I can possibly handle you, Jessica, but not Ellie and Jane. The zombies are coming, and we have to prepare. It's not even that I won't see you. I can be like a sister to you. Older and maybe cooler."

Jessica laughed. "Older, yeah. But cooler? I'm not so sure about that. I mean, you dress like an old woman."

Kelly's eyes opened wide, startled. "What? I do not."

"I saw the dresses in your cupboard. Trust me, old woman." Jessica laughed again.

"Well, maybe once we get things settled, you can help me adjust my wardrobe a bit," Kelly suggested.

"It's going to take a lot, sis." Jessica smiled, and Thomas felt relieved that the girl had acquiesced. He knew that it would make life a whole heap easier all around.

A car entered the driveway and the three girls looked at each other. Thomas tensed, expecting them to attempt something now.

"We've talked among ourselves. If we go, it's together," Jane declared. "We're like sisters."

The other two nodded.

"But if Kelly's my sister..." Jessica started.

"That makes her our sister, dummy," corrected Jane.

Hayley entered the room. "Hi Jack, Thomas. Hey, Kelly."

They greeted her, and Hayley waved to the girls who introduced themselves, and she settled herself on the lounge. The chatter was slow as Hayley drew them out, collected names and dates and locations, and asked about their experiences. Jessica and Ellie were quite open, Jane the only one who didn't share. Thomas wasn't surprised. He had an inkling she'd been through more than she'd even shared with the other two girls, given the hard outer shell she surrounded herself with.

When the girls rose and collected the bags with their items, Thomas felt Kelly trembling beside him. "Jessica's stuff is in the car, downstairs," she whispered, her voice thick with unshed tears, and he felt the pain of her separation keenly. "I left it in there after I went home to gather it all up. I just..."

"I'll get it." Thomas rubbed his hand over hers, hoping it would transfer some of his strength to her.

"Yeah," she whispered.

The girls and Hayley, along with Jack, trooped down the stairs, and Thomas gathered the bags of items from the car Kelly had driven back.

As the girls climbed into the vehicle, their items stored in the trunk, Thomas glanced up to see Kelly on the verandah, arms wound tightly around her waist. He understood her pain. Losing anyone, even on short acquaintance these days, was tough, but she'd already invested in Jessica, and seeing her go... He knew Kelly felt she'd given up. Not that Jessica now saw it that way, but it would take time for Kelly to understand that if wasn't a failure on her part.

The car left the yard, and Thomas turned to Jack. "I'm taking Kelly home. We need a night alone. I need to talk to her. Be there for her."

Jack turned. "I understand. Take it slow. She's been hurt so many times, she's going to be skittish."

All of which Thomas knew.

***

Thomas carried a wine outside to Kelly, and she accepted it with a quiet "thank you" when the thumpa-thump started. Startled, she rose. "What the hell...?"

Thomas shot up from his chair. "That's a chopper."

She turned to him. "What does this mean? Have the zombies... No, they won't know how to fly. The people in charge?" It was like a sucker punch to the belly.

They watched as one became two then four. They came into view, flying low and with intent.

"Get the keys," he growled, and she dropped her tumbler, ignoring the sounds of shattering glass. They piled into the car, and she drove fast, following the line of helicopters toward the waterfront where they landed.

The markings on them denoted them as Australian Air Force, yet she doubted there were many pilots left, and all craft had been grounded after the plague spread like wildfire through the country.

"How the hell did they get here?" she muttered.

They watched as teams disgorged, the uniforms of khaki with dark grey splotches and the unmistakable US Air Force emblazoned on them. Perhaps they're just using existing helicopters? It was all quite confusing.

One man in uniform strode forward. "I'm looking to meet with whoever is in charge. I'm Major Ian McDougall." His accent was clearly American, Kelly thought, and she watched as he held out a hand and Thomas accepted it.

"Major McDougall, I'm Thomas, the head of the local militia, and this is Kelly, my second-in-charge. Our leader, Jack, is home at the moment with his twin daughters. His wife gave birth to their third child yesterday. However, I can take you to him."

The major grunted. "Well, it seems you folks have made quite a settlement here." He looked around. "The zombie infestation isn't as bad as we were led to believe?"

"Not on the island, but the mainland is a different story," Kelly added. "In fact…" Catching sight of Thomas' face, she stopped. "Umm, what are you doing here? I mean, no disrespect but, you know. We've been on our own for a few years now."

The major cleared his throat. "Yes. It's taken us some time to round up a multi-nation force. We've got English, French, and even a few Africans assisting with the task of cleaning up the situation."

"Assisting with cleaning up? I'm not sure I understand."

The major looked at the ground then back up again. "If you could take me to whoever is in charge?"

Kelly wasn't sure she liked not knowing what was going on, but she indicated to the car. Thomas climbed in beside her, and while the major obviously had no liking of being relegated to the back seat, he got in.

"How many are on the island here?" the major asked.

Thomas opened his mouth, and Kelly shot him a look. "Well, I guess that depends—"

"On what you're prepared to tell us," she finished.

Thomas shook his head, but she ignored it.

"We'll take you to Jack, and he can decide whether or not to answer your questions." She could feel the waves of tension coming off the major, and normally she wouldn't act like this, but today? She was tired, frustrated, and sick to death of the garbage they'd all had to deal with in the last couple of years.

"Young lady—"

"That's Kelly to you. Major," she tacked on.

He huffed.

The rest of the drive took place in silence.

Jack waited on the verandah, and they drove in. She was once more thankful his gates were remotely controlled. Parking behind his car, Kelly pulled on the brakes and climbed out. She made her way up the stairs to Jack, who was frowning with a fretting Leanne in his arms. She took the fractious toddler.

"This is Major McDougall," she told Jack. "He says he's part of a multi-national team."

"Kel," warned Thomas, and she turned.

"Don't Kel me, Thomas. How about putting the kettle on? What's wrong with Leanne?" she asked Jack.

"I think it's another tooth," he answered.

"A cold compress," offered the major. "I found with my kids it helps. They suck and bite down, particularly an icy one."

Jack's brow rose. "I think there's one in the freezer, Kel. Addie tends to be on top of all these things."

They trooped inside and assembled at the kitchen table, Kelly holding the little one on her lap, Thomas and Jack flanking her, and the major opposite. I guess it's a show of solidarity. Shame there wasn't much else to laugh about, she thought.

"I realise my arrival is a surprise. To be honest, I didn't quite know what to expect when we landed. The mainland area of Brisbane—" He pronounced it as Brizbayne. "—is riddled. It's going to take months to clear the mess, so I was sent north to see what the status is. We thought we'd start with the islands, thinking they may be easier, and we could move survivors out to them."

Jack remained quiet. Thomas tensed, and she wanted to speak, but the baby was starting to settle so she held her tongue.

"It seems that's not an option here. However, we are after intelligence as to what the situation is over there." He pointed to the mainland.

"Bad," she muttered, and Leanne moved restlessly in her lap.

"Define bad," the major requested, so Thomas began to explain what they knew. The evolution of the zombies, the caging of them. The riotous as the zombies communicated, and the fury of those unable to fight back.

The major clasped his hands. "That marries with what we've learned in Canberra. A task force is to be established in each state to rid the country of zombies. But if what you say is true—that they communicate—it's going to make our task harder. We're going to need locals, guides, and bases. Places that are safe where teams can relax and recuperate. Bases of operations."

Jack quirked a brow. "You're thinking of here?"

The major frowned. "You're established. Have obviously established a food supply system and have the rudiments of—"

"We have enough for our own. We can't feed an army."

The major inhaled. "No. We bring in ships with supplies. Doctors and specialists. Scientists and…"

"And you expect to be housed, I take it?" Thomas enquired.

"If you have room. We can look at your systems, assist with shoring up electrical and plumbing—"

"Upgrade, you mean," Jack said, and she noted the instant the major understood the intent of the comment.

"If that assists, then yes."

Jack steepled his fingers. "I need to talk to Thomas and Kelly. My wife and our leaders. We need two days to consider it."

The major blustered. "Two days?"

Thomas stood. "You heard Jack. We have a series of meetings already planned for the next few days. We are a democratically run island. The decision must be made by the citizens."

The major didn't appear to like the answer, but Thomas moved him out the door.

"I'll be back after I drop him off," Thomas called.

Kelly looked to Jack. "What do you think?"

"It's an offer that's hard to refuse. If they're going to really clean up the mainland, our island is in a key position to benefit from the situation, but…" He shrugged. "I'm one person. This must be discussed with the rest of the islanders. It's too big not to involve them."

Kelly agreed. "I think she's finally asleep." She rose, carried the baby down the hall, and placed her into the crib sitting empty and waiting for her. When she returned, Jack had a coffee waiting. "I'm going to turn into a coffee bean at this rate."

"At least you'll be a good-looking coffee bean." Jack laughed. "But seriously, what do you think?"

"I don't know, Jack. I mean the timing is…" She shook her head. "Amazingly fabulous, but is it too good to be true?"

The sound of the approaching car had her rising. Thomas parked and came inside, settling down beside her. "I got more information. Showed him my police accreditation."

"You're not police anymore," she muttered.

"Nope. But he doesn't know that, and I haven't handed in my badge yet. Haven't really had time. So, the major opened up. They're cleaning things up in Canberra. There's a big farm down there, set up kind of similar to here. People trying to live their lives as best they can, and he's going to organise contact with them next time."

"Anything else?"

"They're winning the war down there. Going to use the experience they had there to tailor how they tackle up here. The mutations aren't unusual either. He said they had some rudimentary communication skills and were capable of working together. There's a militia, and they discovered the source of the initial infection."

Jack jerked beside him. "What?"

"Remember Addie said something about a government conspiracy? She was on the money. Some high-ranking official set up a plan. Inoculate the water source with a water-borne disease, then claim they knew how to fix it. Only thing is it went wrong. That's where the plague came from. They used unsuspecting soldiers to deliver the virus, and the release of the serum to undo it failed. They're trying to find a cure, but so far nothing's taken."

"That's a lot to learn in, what, ten minutes?" Jack drawled.

"Well, I could say I have an honest face, but I refused to let him out until I got enough information. You need to tell the district leaders all this," Thomas urged.

"Yeah. And I need to talk to Addie," he added.

"When is she due to be released?" Kelly enquired.

"Tomorrow morning. They're releasing the baby too. She's feeding well, and while we'll need to check in pretty much daily with the nurse, so long as there's no hiccups, she's good to come home."

"Just in time, huh." Then Kelly giggled. "Well, if you don't need us this evening...?"

Jack looked at her, then Thomas. "Go home. Have a wine. Celebrate. Do something, just get out of here."

Without any further words, Kelly scooped up the keys from where Thomas had slid them on his return, and they left, headed for home.

The drive was quiet. Reflective.

As she parked the headlights shone on the shards of glass where they'd left them.

"I'll clean them up," Thomas offered. "Get yourself another wine. Me too, since I bet mine is full of fruit fly."

Without a word, she left him to clean up and headed inside. Instead of turning right to the kitchen, she moved left toward the bedroom and pulled off her shirt and pants. Slid the underwear from her body and stashed it in the hamper then opened her wardrobe. Inside sat a box, where she'd stuffed it years ago. With shaking hands, she tugged it out.

Once she placed it on the bed, Kelly lifted the lid reverently. Inside was an impossibly sheer gown of gold, trimmed with delicate lace. Aware this was a bold move, she slid the material over her nude body. She'd bought it for him, and tonight it felt right to let it finally have its time.

Turning off all the lights as she made her way through the house, Kelly wondered how Thomas would react. Would he rebuff her and the move she planned to make, or would he understand? Welcome it?

In the kitchen, she found the two wine glasses from her parents' wedding. It seemed right, somehow, that these were the ones she'd choose. The wine, one of the last remaining bottles from her parents' stash, was cool in the fridge where she'd placed it earlier.

The cork slid free with an audible pop and she poured two glasses. Inhaling deeply, Kelly scooped up the glasses and headed for the door, where it lay open.

Stepping outside, Kelly knew the moment Thomas saw her. The jerk of initial reaction then the stillness.

"Kelly?"

"I bought this for you many years ago, Thomas. Tonight... Tonight I want to share it with you." She handed him a glass with a visibly shaking hand.

"I... I don't need wine, Kel. You intoxicate me." The dark timbre of his words soothed the raggedness of her nerves a little.

"You like it?"

"I do." His eyes glinted in the half-light of the moon. "I bought something for you too."

She blinked and felt like the oxygen had once more fled her lungs. "You...you did?"

He nodded and reached into a pocket. "Carried it with me for years. Then I put it in my pocket before the mission, kind of like a good-luck trophy." Uncertainty flitted across his face. "Want to see it?"

"Yeah."

He held out a hand. A jeweller's box, flat and small, filled his hand. OMG. OMG. OMG.

"Open it, Kelly."

She reached for it. Her hands shook as she slid off the lid, unsure if she should expect a ring or what. If he'd bought a ring... She'd surely die, she thought. The top slid away, and she brushed back the paper.

A necklace holding a heart sat in the middle, along with a message.

I'm one of three.

When you're ready so too will they be.

Just like my heart.

"Thomas?"

"I have the ring too. And the earrings. I planned to give the earrings to you on our wedding day. I was just waiting for you to finish school before asking, Kelly."

She burst into tears. "I'm..."

His arms slid around her. "It's okay. I know it was my father's actions that did the damage. One day, I want to be in the position to ask you. For you to say yes and us to build a life."

She could barely stumble to the chair. "I would have said yes. I dreamed of that, Thomas. But afterward, he threatened me."

"I know. Jack was there one time. He told me. I wish he'd rot in hell, but I don't think even hell would want him."

"I wanted tonight to be perfect," she whispered brokenly. "I wanted to surprise you."

He crouched down beside her. "You have, love."

"I wanted to make love with you tonight. By the light of the moon. To begin again, fresh."

Thomas wiped the tears from her cheeks and leaned in. "We can start fresh. Now. Tonight. So long as you're sure." His breath fanned her face.

"I am."

"Then dry your eyes, my love. Come stand under the light so I can admire what has been created for me." He added a mock leer, and she giggled. "That was funny?"

"Oh no, sir. Never funny," she said and batted her eyelashes at him.

"If only we had music," Thomas said.

"We do. I have my phone and some speakers. Sometimes I take them on the boat." She rose. "Let me go get it."

"In a moment," he said and took the necklace from the box. "Wear this. For me."

He moved around behind her, and she knew what he wanted and raised her hair. The act of fastening the necklace was intensely sensual. The whisper of breath on the nape of her neck, the moonlight; it all came together to set a scene where romance and love was the ultimate prize.

Her body warmed, and as she stepped away, she knew there was no turning back. "I'll just be a minute."

Inside the house she took long enough to inhale. The scent of him seemed to hang in the air, and the hunger she'd ignored roared to life. With careful movements, Kelly moved to the kitchen, unplugged the phone from the charger, and gathered the tiny speaker.

As she once more exited the house, her finger pressed on the ID scanner, and she scoured the songs she'd downloaded long ago. A couple of albums featured slow, romantic songs, so she found the first and the strains of saxophone filled the air.

"Hmm, I know that song," he muttered.

"You should. We slow danced to it at your graduation," Kelly answered.

"Ah, yes. I remember that night well." His grin grew.

"Good thing you do," she whispered, moving into his embrace.

Being in his arms was like returning to heaven. She nestled close, remembering the feel of his body from all those years ago, yet it too had changed. He'd filled out a lot. Not fat, but the muscles he'd worked on developing had matured.

The touch of his hand on her back, making lazy circles, was arousing, as was the brush of body against body. With only a single, thin layer clothing her, and his jeans and shirt, there was too much material between them.

"Thomas?"

"Hmm?"

"Would you take off your shirt? Please?"

His hands moved away. She wanted to cry at the loss of connection, but when his fingers found the button on his shirt, she swallowed the sound. Steadily, he popped each button, and she wondered if he had any idea how that studied striptease of his aroused her.

He dropped the shirt to the floor. "Want more?"

Oh God, do I ever! She had to clear her throat. "Ye... Yes. Yes, please."

His fingers dropped a little lower to the buckle of his belt. "You sure?"

"Yes. Totally."

Liquid heat pooled in her belly as he moved the tongue, and released the leather, then he toyed with the button of his jeans.

"Don't stop, Thomas," she implored.

The pressure on the mound between her legs grew, and it took everything she had not to squirm against the sensation of want and emptiness.

He disrobed slowly, igniting her senses in a way no one else had ever done, and finally, clad in only his boxers, and she in the gown, they came back together. This time their mouths fused. His tongue swept deep into the cavern of her mouth, and his hands slid down, finding her hips and tugging her closer.

His erection nudged hard against her belly as they tasted each other properly for the first time in many years.

When he tugged his mouth from hers, they both gasped, and his lips found the sensitive spot behind her jaw and just below her ear. She arched and cried out as his hand covered her breast. A thumb slid over the distended nipple. "I love your breasts, Kel. So soft and yet firm. The tip that puckers a wild raspberry colour."

His other hand caressed her ass, and she squirmed closer, needing more.

"Thomas? I want..."

"Yes, tell me what you want, love. Do you want my fingers to touch you? My mouth to love you, or my cock to fill you?" His words, dark and erotic, ratcheted up her need.

"All. Everything. Fill me. Love me." She could barely speak a coherent sentence now, with the madness descending and her body demanding he complete her as no other man could.

"How do I undo this?" he muttered, looking for a fastener.

Her hand dropped between the cups of the gown. She pushed the two metal pieces together, and suddenly, the gown gaped open, baring her to his view.

Taking control, he slid one strap down. "I want you naked, Kel. I want us both naked so I can fill you up."

With a quick move, she jerked the other shoulder, so the strap also dropped to the ground. "So, you need to take those off then too." And she glanced down, noting the urgent push of his cock against the satin of his boxers.

He tugged them down, and now, skin to skin, they came together. He shoved her hands up and slid his palm flat against her body.

"So fucking beautiful," he moaned, then his lips settled over one breast, his tongue flicking, and her knees gave. Before she could fall, he grabbed her up. "I'm so ready for you, I can't wait," he muttered.

"Don't." And holding onto his shoulders, she slid one leg then the other around his hips and impaled herself. "Oh... Oh God," she muttered.

"I meant... Oh fuck... You're so tight," he ground out. "I meant to use a condom," he groaned against her neck as they vibrated against each other.

"I don't care, Thomas. Just love me."

"I do. I have. I will."

The words echoed in her mind like a vow, until her body, overcome with pleasure, peaked. Her thoughts splintering apart, she held on, riding the pleasure, lost in the maelstrom until, finally, reality returned. She slumped against him, aware he'd tottered to the wall and used it to hold him up.

She slid to the ground. "Wow." She found her way on unsteady legs back to the seat, uncaring of her nakedness.

"Yeah," he muttered as he slid back to his own.

A breeze fluttered, and she shivered, not so much from cold, but as raw nerve endings settled after their wild and frenzied lovemaking.

"You cold?" he queried.

"No. Just...settling, I guess." She turned her face to the moon. "Another clear night. I wonder who else sees this moon?"

"Everyone all over the world." He cleared his throat. "I didn't use a condom."

She nodded. "I know. I don't care, Thomas. If a baby does eventuate, I'll welcome them." Avoiding his gaze during this part of the conversation was tricky, she thought. "I'm done being alone. I don't want to be alone anymore. I want another chance, if you're willing."

His hand slid over hers. "I thought that's what this was about?"

"This..." She paused a moment and pointed to the clothing scattered on the ground. "...was about leaping into the unknown. About taking chances and trusting. I..." She grabbed a strand of hair, tugged, and let the tiny sting centre her. "I trust you. It's me that I find hard to trust, I guess. Knowing who to believe."

He rose and tugged her into his arms. "You can trust me. Trust in us. I'll be here as long as you want me, and when you get sick of me, I'll be like a dog, following you everywhere, sniffing every bush."

Kelly laughed at the stupidity of his words, except they weren't that stupid, were they? "Let's go in," she said and bent down to retrieve the gown and his scattered clothes. When she turned back to get her wine glass, he had both of them in hand.

Entering the house, closing the door, and knowing it was just the two of them? It felt right.

CHAPTER 12

The scent of coffee woke Thomas, and it took a moment to work out where he was. In Kelly's bed. He opened his eyes.

"I brought you a coffee," Kelly said, now covered in an oversized shirt she'd always preferred as night attire.

He shimmied up in the bed, until his back rested against the wall, and took the cup she held out to him, inhaled the aroma. "Life blood." He sighed.

"Uh-huh." She settled beside him, cradling her own cup. "So, uh, what next?"

He knew exactly what she was asking. "We go out. We do the jobs we planned today, then we come home."

He'd never understood the theory behind 'home' before this. Oh, when his mother had been alive and alone, he'd visited regularly, but in his mind, it was 'her place.' After his parents' death he inherited the house they'd lived in, but it didn't appeal to him. It wasn't home.

"Is that what you want? To make this home?" she asked.

Considering her words, he thought over the differences between the two houses. This one had happy times ingrained in the atmosphere. The well-worn carpets an indicator that people had come and gone, lived, laughed, and even grieved in the home. Chairs had sinking cushions, indicating they were used, and areas laid out to encourage interactions and discussions.

It wasn't the cold shell with the picture-perfect furnishings and micro-ensuite because everyone had to have the latest. "You know the house I grew up in. It's...empty."

Kelly took a long moment before replying. "But it's still your home," she said with a gravelly, emotion-laden voice.

"No. It's the house where I grew up. This place," he said as he nodded to the walls, "this is a home. I remember laughing here so many times, learning new skills, and spending happy summer days here. This is what a home is."

"Okay, so do you want to bring some stuff over?" Kelly picked at the bedcovers with her free hand.

"I could. If you want me to." He couldn't explain just how that offer made him feel like his chest was expanding with pleasure. "We could grab them on our way back from the meetings."

"Yes, that makes sense." Reticence now coated her words.

Understanding dawned, and he wanted to swallow his tongue. If this was going to work, he needed to be more aware of her needs. "You could visit with Addie and the babies while I do that, if you'd like."

She deflated, exhaling heavily like a balloon. "I'm not afraid to go, Tom. It's just..."

"I understand, or at least I'm willing to try. I know the house doesn't have good memories for you."

He waited while she sipped her coffee, knew she was taking a moment to clear the confusion from her mind. "No, I'll come with you. I know you're offering me an opportunity to dodge it, and I do appreciate it, but I've got to make changes. Take control of my life instead of letting my fears control me."

"We've got time. We can take as long as you need." He slid the coffee cup onto the table beside the bed. "It's not a splash and dash," he muttered.

Kelly laughed. "You had to bring that up, huh? Even after all these years, when I was so focussed on winning at that competition."

"No, Kel. That's not what I meant. It's more about making sure you know I'll do whatever I need to do to ensure you're comfortable as we move on."

"I know, Tom. I know."

She drank the coffee quietly, and he let her be, aware that every step forward needed to be approached carefully. Once they'd finished their drinks, he rose and waited for her to do the same, feeling off-balance. He'd had more than a few morning-after-the-night-before experiences, but this time, he was hoping this was his last. Was she comfortable with him heading to the bathroom naked? Did she expect him to dress immediately? What was the best plan of action?

Those concerns died away when Kel stripped the shirt from her body as she stood and wandered to the dressing table to gather under-wear. "I'm going to shower. You can join me or go next, what suits?"

Closing his eyes, Thomas sent a silent prayer of thanks for Kelly. Whether she'd known of his concerns, he couldn't say, but with her take-charge attitude, she'd cut through his fears.

They showered quickly, he after her, knowing if they were in the enclosed space, naked and together, he'd likely be unable to control himself. He wanted to get his hands on her again, but today, it wasn't an option as they had to get to Jack and Addie's.

"We don't want to be too early, Tom. Jack was heading out to collect Addie from the hospital and will probably need time to settle the baby. Perhaps we should wait a while?"

Glancing at the clock, he noted it wasn't yet eight. "We can do breakfast, then we really should head over. Do you know what time Addie was likely to come home?"

Kelly shook her head. "Not really, but I would think they would want her out of the hospital as early as possible. When they headed to the hospital, Cherie said the sooner they can get them out, the better."

Settled at the table, with a bowl of cereal and another coffee in hand, the silence stretched. It was companionable and soothing, but before long they'd finished and cleared the table. After a couple of last-minute tasks, they were finally ready to go, and they headed for Tom's car, where he'd parked it days before under the tree.

"I've never seen you drive this one before," Kelly said, climbing into the mid-range SUV.

"I guess I was planning on looking at transferring in the next few months." He'd seriously considered leaving the island, with only Jack and Addie to hold him on the island. With Kelly's withdrawal he'd been spending less time here, until his placement, based on his original request.

Silence stretched. "I didn't realise…"

"It's okay. That was before the plague, then things changed." He shot her a look. "I didn't tell you that to upset you, Kel."

"I know."

The road ahead was empty, but he concentrated on it, as if in peak hour on a Sydney motorway, hands gripping the wheel.

"I made a mess of everything."

"No, Kel. You did what you thought was right. One day, I hope you'll tell me what was said, and why it hurt you so much that you avoided and ignored me for years."

Once more silence reigned, and he was thankful when they swung into Jack and Addie's driveway.

The wail of a new baby split the air, and he couldn't control the grin that covered his face. "Sounds like they're home."

At the door they stopped, the room empty, but the wail louder than it was. The cries of the twins started up, an echo to the strident cry.

Jack hurried down the hall, a harried look on his face. "You're here already."

"Want us to help with the twins, Daddy?" Kelly teased.

"Uh, yeah. If you could. Leanne had a bad night and Fiona's gone out in sympathy."

Kelly zoomed off down the hall, and Thomas eyed Jack. "Feeling a bit overwhelmed?"

"Your time will come, Tom."

His brain reminded him that it might be as soon as nine months away, if she'd got pregnant last night. It now occurred to him that he wouldn't mind that. His mind helpfully supplied a vision of Kelly, her belly distended with his child, and now he hungered for it.

"You alright?" Jack asked.

"Never better," Thomas said with a smile. "Never better."

***

In the babies' room, Kelly cuddled Leanne while Fiona crawled around her legs, and Addie nursed the baby in the rocking chair Jack had found for her.

"So, you're looking happy, Kelly."

"I... We slept together last night." The words tumbled out.

"Ah. And how do you feel?"

Kelly smiled. "I feel great, Addie. But we, uh, didn't, ah...use a condom."

"Oh, okay. So how do you feel about that?" Addie disengaged the baby from her breast and slid the child over her shoulder. The baby responded with a loud belch. Then Addie repositioned her clothes and set the baby to her other breast.

"Does it hurt?" Kelly asked.

"What?"

"Feeding the baby?" She felt a blush rise and ducked her head.

Addie laughed. "Not if it's done right, but I had to learn with the twins. I had sore nipples, and lots of help in the early days, but with help, I got comfortable with the process, which I'm really pleased about now."

"Okay." For the first time, Kelly had real interest in the process of pregnancy and childbirth. Beforehand, any consideration of a future with Thomas and the growing of a family had seemed at some future time.

Addie finished feeding the baby while Leanne sucked on the face washer and Fiona a bottle. The newest member of the family dozed off, and Addie popped her into the newly erected cot, the alarm set up beside it. Addie scooped up Fiona, and with Kelly carrying the now hefty Leanne, the group moved into the lounge.

They settled in the lounge. "Okay, so Addie, you've missed all the excitement," Thomas said.

"If you mean the helicopters, not at all. Two officers came into the hospital last night while you were meeting with the major. Cherie told me about it this morning before Jack arrived. Said they wanted to see the setup, make sure it would be able to cope if they set up a base."

Jack growled. "They should have checked with us first."

Kelly considered Addie's words. "Perhaps, but if the residents here can gain access to other kinds of medical help, the kind we haven't seen since this mess all started, surely that has to be good for the community?"

"I'm not sure it's so much that, Kel. And you're right, it is a good outcome, but if they run over us now, how will we get on if things get really difficult? I mean, will they try to take over the running of the community?" Thomas softened the words by rubbing his thumb over their intertwined hands.

Kelly was unreasonably aware that both Addie and Jack had noticed the gentle caress, but she had no intention of pulling away. "Hmm. You make a good point. So, with everything we've learned—"

"Hang on," interrupted Addie. "What happened on the mainland? I know you brought two young girls back, but what happened over there?"

Thomas tensed. "It's a mess, Addie. Worse than when Jack and I led the teams to get Cherie and her family over here." He pulled away and clasped his hands together between his knees, as if taking a second to gather his thoughts. "There are new, stronger zombies, and they're even more dangerous than those we've faced before. I can't stress that enough. We know some who tried to get through the gates to the bridge were evolved, but not like these. We know they had some limited communications, but based on what we saw, it appears that they're now planning as well. Working together. Just before we came back, we went to the top of the Osprey building. There's a compound where the zombies are being kept prisoner. They were being herded by people in military style vehicles. Just like a militia to be frank. They were prodding the ones they'd let free, trying to get them back into the compound when they charged. The zombies mutinied against the actions."

"What?" Addie sat upright in her seat. "So, you're telling me—"

"That's not all, Addie. We saw them swimming. Not well, but this is a newly acquired skill. We've seen now what they are capable of learning, in those few minutes on top of the Osprey building. Just like the communication and rudimentary planning. Once they gain the skill, they practice and perfect it."

"Oh..." Addie paled and laid a hand on her chest. "That's bad."

"Really bad," echoed Kelly.

"That's why we have to meet with the divisional leaders today. Explain what we've learned and make sure everyone turns up tomorrow to the community meeting. We need to make decisions. Getting the military on side is only one part of the fight though. We're independent. Democratic. We need the people to agree with this, and there's less than twenty-four hours," he added, checking his watch, "to build a case the islanders will accept."

"I don't know. They may have questions," Kelly said.

"We have all day, if need be, Kel. We answer them fully and frankly. We need their co-operation, and I don't think we'll get that if we only tell them part of the story," Jack responded.

"What time will they be here, Jack?" Addie asked.

"In about an hour, so now we have to craft how we talk to them. There are a few older folks who won't be keen to rock the boat. They like the safety of the island and that we're caring for each other and no one is going without. I think the younger ones will mostly be looking for autonomy given the fact we've been self-governing and self-sustaining since the beginning."

"We could look at asking for some exemptions, rather like Norfolk Island used to do before all this. Tax relief, restrictions on travel to and from, that sort of thing. Has anyone got any idea if they were affect-ed?" queried Kelly.

"No, I don't, but I think that's an excellent idea. We'll be looking to bargain for freedoms and sureties from the government going forward." Jack jotted it down on the notebook he'd lifted from the floor beside his seat.

"I think everyone would like that," Thomas said as his hand squeezed hers.

"If we're going to be a base of operations, the hospital needs staff. Doctors, a working theatre, and Cherie was saying some medications are getting low. Since she and her husband are split between the prac-tice and the hospital, they're getting a little thin too," Addie added.

"Been working, even in hospital, have you?" Jack wound his arms around his wife. "But that's the kind of information we need to know. We should ask what other concessions—"

"That might be a way to get the islanders involved, if we ask them in the open meeting tomorrow." Thomas grimaced. "I suppose there won't be a job for me after all."

Jack shook his head. "Not at all. They're going to need to know who's who. Where to go. What the situation is. Local intelligence, and that's what you offer."

"I just..." Thomas muttered, and Kelly felt the sudden tension in him.

Kelly squeezed his hand. "We need authorised personnel to liaise with the military. They're not going to care that you resigned from the police force. You're capable, knowledgeable—"

"And as the Island's democratically elected head, the official liaison between us and the military," Jack answered. "Now, let's get this down while the baby's asleep. Kelly's offered to type up the notes so we can circulate them at the meeting later."

CHAPTER 13

Waiting on the waterfront for the choppers to arrive, Thomas scanned the horizon. Beside him waited Kelly and Jack. They'd all agreed Addie would stay home with the children, given there'd already been a huge amount of disruption, and with a tiny baby to care for, any rest was welcome.

"Think they'll go for our plan?" Tom queried, watching the large aircraft grow in size as the noise became gradually louder. He wondered what they saw. Do they think we're uneducated hicks living on some island, or will they accept us as peers?

"I have no idea, frankly. My gut says they need us, but who knows? Military types tend to be a law unto themselves," Jack answered.

Winds buffeted, and they retreated further up the beach, covering their eyes as sand whipped around them. Rotors slowed until they finally ceased. A pilot, Tom guessed, climbed from the front as the side door slid open. The major climbed out and headed in their direction. Today he was dressed more formally, and an entourage followed.

"Jack. Thomas. Kelly." He shook hands and introduced his offsiders, "Mary, my official aide. Frank, a military photographer. And Lance." No description was given of Lance's role, but the other two treated him deferentially, so Tom had an inkling something was going to go down. "So, where do you plan—?"

"Come up the beach a bit, major. We've erected a tent for the meeting, and I've got food and drink in there too." Jack ushered them beyond the stand of trees to where a large, white gazebo had been put up just that morning.

Jugs of water and juice waited on tables. Water glasses gleamed beside the jugs, which streamed with condensation. There were plates filled with pastries and fruits, and further over, small savoury quiches waited. The tablecloth was a pristine white.

The tables they'd chosen were heavy wooden with large chairs, and on the floor, they'd had carpet laid down.

The major scanned the room, quirked an eyebrow, then advanced to the table.

"We have coffee and tea too, should you prefer it," Kelly offered.

"You can present a spread like this, even though you're effectively cut off from the world?" the major queried.

"We are not without resources," Jack pointed out mildly, and the major frowned.

It heartened Thomas that their intended plan, to show the major that they needed the military far less than the military needed them, to self-sustain, was clearly successful. Anything to drive home that they'd found a way to cope and keep out the zombies.

At the meeting yesterday the divisional heads had agreed to the plan. After all, once it had been laid out, benefits of any concessions they might draw outweighed the concerns of those not wishing to return to 'the old way of doing business' as one man had pointed out.

"But why do we need them to come? We've made a life now. They'll want to take over, make decisions and rules from Brisbane again," a woman called from the back.

Thomas shifted from one foot to the other. "It's not just a case of them taking over. We don't want them to do that, but there is a threat looming, one that could undo everything we've achieved."

"But how do we know this?" she called out. "I mean, you're telling us—"

"I've seen them! I've seen them swim, and I've..." Jessica shot to her feet, and Thomas smiled, aware the young girl wanted to participate in the discussions. If the young were on board, and they could sway those who saw opportunities, they might just have a chance.

"Thanks, Jessica." He nodded, and the young girl's lips drew tight, then she sat down again. "Jessica was rescued by Kelly from the zombies. Kelly saw them too. She reported what she saw to us, and we took a team over, rescuing another two girls in the process. During our time there, we saw the situation. There's militia over there, controlling the zombies. But from what we saw, even their control is slipping. We barely got away, but not before we saw, with our own eyes, the development. Not only can they swim, but they communicate and are planning."

Gasps came from within the building on all sides.

"Then what we did with the bridge and holing up here..." a woman to his left called out.

Thomas nodded. "Yes. That's why the timely arrival of the military gives us an opportunity which didn't exist before. One we should grab with both hands, people. But we can make it work for us."

While the meeting had dragged out for over four hours, in the end, they had the majority of the populace on side.

"You make a good point, Jack. But I know your kind. You want us to agree to things, and it depends on whether I can give them." The major settled at one end of the table. Thomas recognised the power play and smiled when Jack took the other end. Kelly and himself settled in the seats on Jack's right, and the military crew on the left.

Notepads and pens waited. A photocopier had been dragged down and slid onto a desk, which had been manhandled down too. And waiting nearby was Tam, who'd take the minutes of the meeting on the laptop.

"Leaving nothing to chance, huh?" the major said.

Jack smiled, and for a moment, Thomas thought he saw a predatory gleam in his friend's eye. "No. I'm representing the citizens of the island. They rely on me to get this right."

The major gave a small laugh. "Fair enough."

Mary, his aide, distributed an agenda, and as Thomas looked down, he noted the words 'no in principle agreement is to be entered into today' emblazoned across the bottom of the page.

The negotiations began, the major asking, Jack countering, and Kelly or himself sometimes supporting the discussion with facts and anecdotes. After two hours, they took a break. They'd chosen the location for access to bathroom facilities, which an outdoor crew had scrubbed until they shone. Once again, the luxuries were laid on—thick, fluffy towels, artisan soaps, and so on.

Thomas overheard Mary mentioning to Lance, "These guys must live well. Did you see their bathrooms?"

Lunch consisted of freshly caught prawns and fresh fish, thanks to Kelly, a garden salad picked just this morning, and soft bread rolls the baker had whipped up this morning, along with the pastries they'd enjoyed earlier.

Three staff—a chef and two waiters from a now defunct restaurant—ensured the meals were perfectly cooked and served, offering discreet service to the table then clearing everything away.

"You make your point well, Jack," the major said with a laugh at the end of the meal. "But your requests are not easy to grant. I can't just wave my hand and—"

"We know that, major. But as you can see, we are capable of running our own show. You need us far more than we need you. We've given you a list of what we believe you can do for us, just as much as we've offered housing, guides, and even a liaison officer. What we are seeking, though, is a level of autonomy into the future from the government. Tax relief for our residents. I appreciate the government will need to consider them, but let's put it this way. As you yourself have said, there are few settlements on the mainland with the kind of resources we have. They may be bigger but not have access to the kinds of service we do. The location here, it's harder for an incursion to take place. Not impossible, but we can patrol it. The government may be in disarray, but we are not. We have a secure location, food, specialists. Can they offer you security for your base? And even if they can, are they able to do that now or will you need to bring in supplies, buildings? Erect lookout structures?"

"You're quite right, of course. We can go back and make certain representations on your behalf," he agreed.

"Why not bring them here, in person, on your next visit?" Kelly said. "Then they can see for themselves. We can meet with them personally. Show them the benefits of allowing us to recover quickly."

Thomas' chest puffed a little further out. She was holding her own in the conversations, offering suggestions that increased the chances of them achieving the outcome they all desired.

"Alright then. Can you whip me up a list of your requests?" the major asked, and Jack smiled.

Tam rose and carried a manilla folder over, inside a list of their requests and suggestions as crafted the day before at the public meeting. She handed the folder over. "We prepared this earlier, in case you wanted it."

The major harrumphed and opened the folder. "Well, it appears you're not only prepared but—"

"We are not without resources or capabilities, major." The words weren't so much a threat as a reminder, and the major nodded.

"I'll talk to my superiors and the government officers. In the meantime, we'd like to place a small contingent here now. If that's acceptable?"

Jack smiled. "Of course. We have some buildings we've completed the refurbishment of, so there's apartments ready."

"There's ten men and three women. They could, of course, share—"

Kelly opened the notebook and scanned. "I've got a list of forty-two current apartments available. I expect they will also require transportation?"

"I... Yes, that would be acceptable."

Thomas could tell he hadn't expected them to be able to house them on short notice. He'll soon learn.

"Great. Now, is there anything else, major?" Jack enquired.

Thomas had to work to control the smile as his friend once again took the lead in the negotiations. He'd never have thought Jack a leader prior to this situation, but in the last months he'd not only grown into the role, but made it his own.

"No, Jack. I think that's all." The major stood, his entourage following. "Lance will remain here. He's our strategist and will need to meet with—"

"We'll make the arrangements for him to meet with those appropriate, major. When do we expect you to return?" Thomas enquired.

"I'll need a few days. Lance will be in touch with me. We've got shielded comms devices," he said absently.

Tam slid away from the desk, the hum of the printer loud. "Jack?"

He turned to the woman in her thirties. "The minutes?"

"Just printing now. Two sets for the major, and I'll make another for—"

"Negotiations are considered confidential," the major blustered.

"They are for our records. As and how information requires dissemination, we'll do so in an appropriate manner," Jack soothed as Tam handed over the carefully printed pages.

"Alright then," the major said and turned, his group following.

Jack, Thomas, and Kelly followed through the door of the gazebo and as far as the barrier trees, watching the major talk animatedly with his crew. Men and women who waited by the craft picked up their heavy bags and moved out of the way of the choppers, and Lance reached in, grabbing out a similar pack. Several other airmen piled boxes on top while the three of them watched.

"What do you think is in the boxes?" asked Kelly.

"I'd guess a radio, probably a camera for collecting intelligence, and who knows what else?" Jack murmured. "They'll want to be collecting as much information on us now as they can. Probably looking to see if we actually are as self-sufficient and capable of governing ourselves as we've presented."

"Well then, let's make sure we're better than expectation," said Kelly. "I have a feeling if the major sees an opening, he'll take every advantage he can."

Thomas had to agree with her sentiments.

***

Kelly dragged the final net in, turning the large wheel manually while Thomas waited the hold. It was shades of younger years, when he'd helped Kelly and her father with the catch.

"Kel, bring it in," Dad called from the cockpit, clearly satisfied that the hours of trawling the sea had collected enough fish for this catch.

She wound the large wheel, ropes groaning under the pressure, until soon, she could see the tip of the net emerging from the water. Her father refused to update to a mechanical retraction device, simply reminding her that 'mechanical is all well and good, but when it fails on the water, how do you fix the issue?'

It was hot, hard work. Her muscles ached as she dug deep for the strength to complete her task, and though dawn hadn't passed all that many hours ago, sweat trickled down her clothes, between her breasts, and prickled her skin.

"God, I wish he'd change his mind about the wheel," she muttered.

"I can hear you, Kel," he called from the front, and she grimaced.

The large arm, which the ropes securing the nets hung over, now acted like a lift as the woven nylon enclosure, filled with fish, rose up. Securing the wheel, she scurried to the side and released the arm.

"Get it, Thomas. Bring it to the hold," she called, and Tom moved, sure of step on the slippery deck.

"It's in," he called and bent down to release the codend so the fish dropped into the shallow hold.

Kelly moved with speed to grab the now free hanging net, swung the arm back and fastened it, while her father cut the engine and clambered down the short ladder to join them.

It didn't take them long to sort the juveniles from the fish they needed, de-heading as they worked, the sharp knife slicing cleanly through skin and bone. "Get 'em back in the water quickly, Thomas," Kelly's father urged. "We want them to grow up big and juicy. To have lots more fish for us to catch." Even as he spoke, he was dragging the good catch into plastic tubs, sorted by type, and soon, that task too was completed.

"Just like old times," Thomas called, and Kelly laughed. The spirit of her father close now, to her mind.

Thomas hadn't lost his touch either; the grace in his movements, the sure moves as he released the fish, it brought back memories.

Once they were both huddled over the sorting table, she smiled. "You're still good at this, Tom."

"I did it enough during the summers that I'd often see it in my sleep."

She snorted. "Well, you better keep going awake." She laughed and returned to sorting and sifting.

"Your dad never upgraded then?"

"No. Even up to the end he said if something went wrong mechanically, we'd be stuck. He put in too many hours trawling to be caught out, he said. But there's definitely days when I wish he'd invested."

They worked in silence until the catch was cleared. Then, after shoving the fish into the refrigerated area, he followed her up to the cabin.

Glancing around, Kelly realised that she really was comfortable here, although sometimes she regretted giving up her dream of interior design.

"Do you wish you'd gone to university?" he asked, and she started, wondering if he'd somehow read her thoughts.

The engine chugged away as she piloted the boat. "Sometimes. I think back now and wonder if fate wasn't nudging me though. I mean, I didn't intend to stay here, fishing for the rest of my life, but Mum died, then Dad had the heart attack. After the plague, well, there wasn't anyone else, and I was doing useful stuff." She shrugged.

"But do you intend to do this until you retire?" He indicated to the boat, the open water.

She knew what he meant. After all, it wasn't exactly the dream job of white net curtains and papers and paint she'd envisioned for herself.

Her hand found a chocolate bar under the wheel, one she'd stashed ages ago. The covering was battered, but she'd eaten old ones before, and without another thought, Kelly tore it away, as hunger left her stomach lurching, and bit deep into the gooey treat.

The chocolate was old and crumbly, the nougat strangely tangy. It's only old. Nothing wrong with it, she thought, as she considered his question. What exactly did she want to do with the rest of her life if the plans they'd made came to pass?

"Oh, God no!" She glanced in his direction. "But I don't know quite what I will do once things return to some kind of normality. I've learned I don't necessarily want to be in an office, and after years away from school, I don't think I could manage university now. The idea of being trapped inside a classroom..." Kelly shuddered. "Not the me I am now."

"But you want something else?" he pushed, and she wondered what he was thinking.

"Yes, I want something else. I mean, I don't know if I could get rid of the boat, because that would be like telling Dad I don't..."

"Why give up the boat? You could lease it out," he urged.

"I could, but there'd have to be someone to lease it to." But the seed was taking root. Train someone who would look after the vessel. They could fish, but she'd be free to follow her own dream, if only she knew what it was.

"Kel?"

Thomas' quiet comment broke through her introspection. "Uh, what?"

He pointed. "What's that?"

In the distance something bobbed up and down, clinging to a log. She chugged closer and peered through the binoculars beside her. "Oh fuck!" she breathed. "It's a zombie."

CHAPTER 14

Thomas squinted through the windscreen. "You're sure?"

Kelly silently passed him the binoculars. "Look for yourself," she urged.

The binoculars allowed him to peer across the distance.

"Oh fuck," he muttered. They thought they had more time, but clearly the zombies were advancing quicker than anyone had expected.

"Do you think this is a one-off?"

"I don't know, Kel, but we need to get back and tell Jack. If there's one..." He didn't dare finish the sentence, because the thought of multiples of these abominations on the water, heading in their direction, was downright horrific.

"We need to tell Lance too," Kelly added.

"We see who we've got that can get on the water, send out men with rifles." His mind whirred, coming up with immediate scenarios, but no matter what he thought up, if they'd managed to find a way to traverse the water between the mainland and them... "If one gets across, pretty soon another will too."

They just didn't have the manpower to patrol and combat this kind of incursion. Hell, he didn't think even the Australian navy would have in the past.

"How quickly can we get to the jetty?" he asked.

Kelly's eyes rolled, the way they always had when calculating something. "If I open her all the way up, maybe twenty minutes? But that's going to chew the fuel reserves."

He knew she wanted to conserve as much as possible, but right now speed was of the essence. "Open her up, Kel. We've got to get back and let Jack know. Then you and I head out in the Mariana." He named the South Bay vessel, and she nodded.

"Who else do we bring with us on the boat?" she asked.

"Lance."

"But I thought—" She wrinkled her nose as she poured on the power, the boat lurching on the waves as they hurried at full speed back to the dock.

"He's going to be useful to us. But first, we need to let Jack know. He's got the lists we made up, so he and Tam can get the others on the boat. We give him the location, you did note it, right?"

"This isn't my first time." She lifted the notepad where she'd scribbled the details. "I wrote it down after I handed you the binoculars," she called, the engine making a loud droning noise.

Soon enough they chugged up to the jetty, and he marvelled at the skill she had at mooring. The ropes were finally attached, and she jumped off the boat, and they hurried to the road. It was still a reasonable distance, maybe ten minutes at a walk, but they both felt the urgency, so they jogged to the house. Addie was outside on the verandah feeding the baby.

"What's wrong?" she asked as they hurried up the driveway.

"We need to borrow the car, Addie. It's an emergency," called Thomas.

While she didn't ask what, and grabbed the keys and flung them to him, he knew she wanted the details.

"I'll explain later, or Jack will. Right now, we need to get to his office. Thanks!" he yelled.

They climbed into Addie's old car, and he reversed it, thankful Jack had insisted that the cars be regularly maintained. While the office wasn't too far from the water's edge, it made more sense to drive. They made it to the office in under five minutes, and they piled out. The door was open, denoting 'library session' was on, so he and Kelly dashed down the hall to Jack's office.

He and Tam were poring over a spreadsheet as they hurried in. "Jack? Good thing you and Tam are here. We've got a problem. We were coming in on the trawler when we saw something on a log, floating."

Jack waited, clearly frustrated at the interruption. "And?"

"It's a zombie, Jack. Alive and floating and headed in our direction," Kelly said. She thrust the notebook at him. "This is the location."

"Fuck me," he muttered. "You're absolutely sure?"

Blood pumped in Thomas' veins, a thrum of adrenaline. "Totally. Kel had binoculars and we used them to check."

"You're sure it was alive?" Jack queried.

"Yeah," added Kelly. "It looked at us. I was sure it knew who we were. But if there's one..." She gulped, and Thomas reached out to grab her hand.

"We need the boat teams up and out. They need to begin urgent patrols. We have to stop them before they make the island. Otherwise..." Thomas let the words hang in the air.

"Yeah. How long ago?" Jack asked, rubbing his brow.

"Maybe thirty or forty minutes ago. We know they can swim, Jack. We know they're planning." Kel's voice held a thread of hysteria, and Thomas rubbed her palm, hoping it would calm her.

"I know." Jack turned to Tam who had a pale face and shook slightly. Thomas felt sorry for the woman. Her husband had been killed by a zombie earlier in the plague, and now she was front line, assisting with the defence of their island. "Get onto the teams, Tam. Send them out." He turned back to Thomas and Kelly. "What's your plan?"

"We're taking the South Bay out. I'll destroy the zombie before it makes it to the island. Then we'll patrol, see what we can see. If there are any others, we'll hopefully find them."

Not that they'd be sure. Not until all the zombies had been eliminated was there any assurance of safety.

"We've got Addie's car, so we'll head back to your place," Thomas called as they retreated.

"Leave it at the jetty. I'll grab it later, or better yet, take it home. I'll arrange for the trawler to be cleared and cleaned. You can pick it up once you've completed your task."

"Fine," called Thomas.

As if the urgency telegraphed itself, the people in the library parted the way, allowing them to exit, though they watched the two as he urged Kelly out of the building.

"Thomas?" Now when Kelly spoke, there was a hint of the self-assured Kelly again.

"Yes, love?" He stuck the key in the ignition and pulled out of the parking lot.

"I hate zombies, and when this is done, I want my ring. I'm not waiting any longer."

His thoughts fractured. "Ring?"

"Yes. The one to match my necklace."

He glanced at Kelly again, his attention divided between the road and her. "I thought we were going to take this slow?"

"Hmm," she said, plucking at her shirt. "I did too, but I also know life is pretty precarious. I mean, what's the chance of finding a single zombie on the water, heading for the island—"

"Damn it," he yelled as he swerved to avoid a dog running along the road and the car jerked. "We should talk about this later," he growled, realising the danger of having a highly emotional conversation while they hurried to get back to Kelly's house.

Kelly remained silent in the seat beside him, and he couldn't tell if it was because she was angry, or she agreed, or what. The whole situation felt pretty damned farcical.

***

Kelly knew she'd thrown him for a loop when she'd demanded the ring. That made her wince, because she had, hadn't she? It wasn't even that she wanted to push him into a position he wasn't ready for. She knew he cared. Thomas wasn't a 'love them and drop them after sex' kind of guy. The moment they'd made love, it had clicked into place in her mind.

He still loved her. Yes, he'd told her, but he wouldn't push her. Seeing that zombie? It slammed home again that their chances of a happy ending were getting slimmer by the day. As the zombies continued their evolution, they brought more of humanity into danger.

Climbing from the car after he'd parked it, she kept her silence, well aware he felt frazzled and discomforted by her words. In truth, she'd loved him all along. There hadn't been any question, but she'd had to come to terms with and overcome her own fear. She'd shied away from that until recently. The words she'd uttered had simply been the conclusion of that journey and the start of the next.

They hurried over the sandbank and down to the jetty where she'd moored the South Bay craft. They climbed in, and once again, she thanked the forethought of immediately refuelling when they'd berthed it. In the tiny hold, Tom had stashed several firearms, and though that in and of itself filled her with misgivings, even if they were in a lockbox, it also made sense now.

She ignited the engine after casting off, and they pulled away, initially at a slow speed, but gradually increasing. In the car she'd been watching the tidal flow, and if her calculations were vaguely correct, the zombie would be heading on a south-southeasterly direction. Settled in the captain's chair, she opened the throttle and arrowed the boat to the vicinity of where she expected it to be. The hull cleaved through the water, spray flying into the air behind them, so that within minutes she could throttle back. The angry thrub, thrub, thrub of the engine echoing in the silence.

"Can you see anything?" Kelly demanded of Thomas, and he shook his head.

Her guts twisted. What if she'd calculated badly? They might miss it. The zombie could—then on the horizon she noted a blob. "Over there," she breathed and turned the boat.

They moved closer. Kelly, more than aware that it would be all too easy to endanger themselves, kept what she hoped was a reasonable distance. She stared and knew Thomas did too. It was a zombie. A large male, like the one they'd seen earlier, only it wasn't the same zombie. This one was missing a hand and the damage to his jaw was clearly old. Yet, here he was, in the water, heading in the direction of the island.

"Shit," said Thomas as he lifted the firearm. The shot ricocheted, and the zombie jerked, the hand holding onto the wood releasing, the pole rolling, and the zombie slid beneath the waves.

"Did you...?" She needed to know for certain if he'd hit the zombie in the head.

"Direct hit," Thomas said and exhaled. "But now we need to find our zombie. Then keep up our patrol. See if there's others and deal with them too."

"I don't..." How could she tell him she didn't know where to begin?

He moved forward and cupped her chin. "It's okay to be frightened, Kel. I am too. I don't want to lose the opportunity of us, but I also don't want to rush because we're frightened. We deserve better than that, because we were both victims of my father. I want us to take our time, enjoy being together."

Tears burned. "I'm sorry, Thomas, I didn't mean to push you into a commitment you're not ready for." And she meant it.

He laughed. "I'm ready, Kel. Have been for years but..." He stilled and she turned, looking in the direction of what he'd seen.

"Over there?" She pointed.

"Over there," he agreed, and she moved away, took control once more of the boat as he settled into the seat, keeping watch as they closed on the floating debris. And there, in the centre, was the zombie they'd seen earlier.

It grinned at them and roared, the sound loud. A mouth full of sharp, grey-green teeth betrayed the fact that it was an older zombie, though the musculature assured her it was a male who'd been in the peak of fitness, with biceps and triceps tinged with the oozing green of decay. Motoring nearer, the stink of it filled the air, and she saw clearly for the first time, the legs, bones jutting out, as skin had split in reaction to the biological changes.

Thomas took aim and squeezed the trigger. The creature jerked away, the bullet grazing flesh which split and splattered into the air. The stink even more stomach churning now.

He aimed and fired again, and this time hit the creature. It howled but held onto the debris, paddling one-handed in their direction.

"Thomas?"

"Stay still," he commanded, and she held the boat steady. The third ping hit dead centre. The face exploding into a mass of gore. The body jerked and rolled, though the hand remained embedded in floating wood. "Can you get closer, Kel?"

She nodded and moved the vessel fractionally.

He peered over the side, then finally Thomas breathed out. "We got him. He's dead."

"That's two, Thomas."

Reaction started to set in, and she shook as the realisation of the precariousness of their position hit home. It wasn't like earlier. Before they knew better they'd been working on an understanding of what was, unlike now. Terror surged because her brain was painting ugly images of zombies attacking Addie and the kids. In her own home... The idea that they might taint her sanctuary was horrifying and gut freezing.

The sudden rise of nausea took her by surprise, and she barely made the side of the boat before vomiting. Thomas was there in an instant, holding her safe, brushing her hair away. "It'll be okay, love," he whispered as she slumped to the floor.

"Will it? Or is our future, however long it's going to be, dogged by the zombies?" She closed her eyes, hating the weakness of her voice and the shakes that captured her. Would her life ever be quiet again?

She heard him squat beside her. "I'm taking you home," he muttered and raised her, even though she tried to fend him off with 'I'll be fine.' But once he lifted her in his arms, she clutched tight, burrowed into him, and let the warmth of his body ward off the sudden chill surrounding her.

Thomas settled her into his seat, fastened the seatbelt, and took up the captain's chair. She slumped back, weak and dizzy, and let him motor the boat home, but each choppy wave sent a flash of queasiness through her belly. She had to concentrate to ward off the lurching of her stomach but was grateful when he tied them up at the jetty.

Her legs felt like jelly, all wobbly and without strength, but when he asked if she could make the house, she nodded. It wasn't too many steps after that when Kelly realised making the house would be an effort. Sweat coated her face, and she knew Thomas was concerned.

"Kel, maybe I should go get Cherie?"

"No. I'll be fine," Kelly croaked, feeling anything but.

Having Cherie come out here though would be overkill, and besides, it was probably one of those nasty bugs that kids always shared, right? She'd probably caught it from one of Addie's trio, but she'd barely finished the thought before another wave struck, and she staggered to the bathroom and was violently ill again.

Slumping on the floor, stomach muscles screaming and feeling like she'd die, Kelly glanced up at Thomas. "I think I should head to bed. If you could find me a bucket?"

"Shower first, so you at least feel a little fresher," he urged and helped her to divest herself of the clothing she'd been wearing since long before dawn.

The warm water sluiced over her skin, and while it didn't settle the constant roil of her belly, she did feel a little more human afterward.

Thomas had ratted out one of her old sleepshirts, and she let him dress her, feeling ridiculously weak and child-like. When she was settled in bed, a weak tea on the bedside table and bucket on the floor, he waited at the door. "I need to see Jack, and I'm getting Cherie. Will you be okay for a while when I go?"

She nodded. "Yeah. I'm going to take a nap," she muttered and curled over the chills returning.

He must have come back into the room, because she felt the touch of his hand against her forehead. Heard his quiet, "Hmm."

Sometime later, she was sure she heard him leave. It was all rather hazy now, and she let herself drift as her stomach continued the pitch and roll, and now her head ached. The flu or stomach bug, whatever it was, had come on quick, she thought before drifting into an uneasy sleep where zombies reached for her, their growls filling the air.

She woke, stomach cramping, head aching, to see night had fallen and Thomas ushering Cherie into the room.

"And what do we have here?" the doctor enquired.

Kelly sat up with a start, and immediately the rise of bile began.

She barely found the bucket in time before the meagre contents of her insides squeezed up and out once more.

***

Thomas waited outside the bedroom door, wondering what the hell was taking so long. Even as he hovered, the sound of an engine grew nearer, and he headed to the front door. Jack entered. "How is she?"

"Still with Cherie," Thomas answered. He'd briefly dropped in to let Jack know he had information, but Addie and he were busy, and to be honest, Thomas had just wanted to get home before Cherie arrived. As it was, she'd caught up and followed him all the way from Jack's.

"Addie won't come in. She's going to drive home in her car when we're done, but is worried if what's wrong with Kelly is contagious."

The bedroom door opened, and Cherie stepped out in time to hear the last words. "Oh, I don't think so. Looks to me like a simple case of food poisoning. She'll be right in a few days but needs to rest and probably shouldn't be alone, Thomas. Not at this point anyway," she added with a smile.

Jack sighed. "Okay, that's good news, I guess?"

Cherie smiled widely. "It's better than the alternative." She shuffled out the door, but then popped her head back in. "Oh, and Jack? I want to see you and Addie next week. Let's say Monday morning, shall we? When you have time, drop in." With that, she was gone.

"You need to report, Tom?"

"Two zombies on planks. They're not close to the beach yet, but they've worked out a way to breach the water barrier, Jack. We didn't see any more, but—"

"I've got the other teams out scanning now. The status of the zombies you did see?" Jack looked out the door and to the large mound separating the house from the water.

"Gone. Dealt with."

Jack nodded. "Good. Okay then, you're both down for a couple of days. When Kelly's able, though, we'll need you both on the case." He straightened and headed for the door. "Find whatever caused her to get sick and get rid of it. The last thing we need is our best people out with food poisoning." Then Jack too was gone.

Thomas closed the door and padded back to the bedroom. Kelly was slowly sipping on orange liquid in a glass, still very pale but a little less shiny with sweat. "Cherie gave me an injection and put this in a glass of water. Said I need to get this down, then do it all again in a couple of hours," she croaked.

"Are you feeling any better?" He settled down on the side of the bed.

She kept herself still as if attempting to ward off a further bout of vomiting. "A little, but my stomach is still kind of dodgy," she breathed, then sniffed. "You might like to have a quick shower," she said and slid a finger under her nose.

"Oh, right." He shot up off the bed. "I'll go shower now, then make some dinner. Do you..." Then he considered his words. "No, I don't suppose you do."

He hustled out quickly but not before he heard her sigh loudly.

Attending to his own needs didn't take long, and a quick meal of eggs on toast filled his belly. Washing up the pan and plate, he considered the kitchen.

The house had been a haven for him during those years he and Kelly had been together. More than once he'd sat here at the kitchen table, eating a meal with her parents. He'd completed his application to the police academy here too, and there'd been boardgames on wet days.

Everything about the house was welcoming, but he remembered Kelly's mother grousing about the linoleum of the floor.

"You want me to cook you dinners, but the kitchen is falling down about my ears. I've asked more times than I care to think of, for you to do something about this flooring."

"I have," Kelly's father answered. "I bought a mat, and after dinner, Thomas, Kelly, and I are going to move the table and chairs and put it down."

Kelly's mother rolled her eyes. "And you think that's going to do the job?"

He smiled widely. "Well, at least until we have to change the mat in twenty years," Kelly's father answered before crowding in on Kelly's mother and sliding a hand around her waist. "Come on, love. Where's your sense of adventure?" He winked at Thomas and gave a nudge of his head.

Kelly slid her fingers into Thomas' grasp. "Let's go for a walk," she said.

He remembered that walk fondly.

He asked Kelly if her parents would be kissing, and she rolled her eyes. "Dad can't keep his hands off Mum at the best of times, so yes, I'd say it's a safe bet to think that."

He stopped Kelly, turned her in his arms. "Reckon we'll be like that in twenty years?"

She laughed and reached up to kiss him.

So many years on, and he wondered how her parents would react if they knew about him and Kelly. Would they approve?

He tiptoed into the bedroom. Kelly was lying on her side, facing the wall. He quietly dragged off his clothes, sliding on the sleep shorts he'd picked up, and settled into the bed beside her, his arm wrapped gently around her waist.

"Finally," she muttered. "Now I can go to sleep," she said before snuggling in and drifting off. He held her in the moonlight, letting his worry melt away with awareness.

CHAPTER 15

Kelly climbed behind the wheel of the car. Four days of recuperation and finally Cherie had given her the all-clear, 'so long as you take it slow.'

Tiredness dogged her, but she was determined to get back into the game.

She and Thomas would take the trawler out tomorrow, but they'd have a new offsider. Dan had been a postman, delivering parcels until the plague put him out of work. Since then, he'd floated between the reconstruction works and labouring in the gardens, but when he'd heard that Kelly and Thomas needed someone to assist with the trawler, he'd been the first to volunteer.

As she parked by the house, she saw the ancient motorbike sitting alongside Thomas' sleeker car.

Traipsing up the mound and down to the jetty, she noted two people on the boat, one working with grace and fluidity, the other checking and asking questions before completing a task.

"Hey, Dan. Great to have you aboard," she called.

"Oh, hi captain," he called, and she grinned.

"No one calls me that. It's Kelly, or hey you."

Dan nodded, then Thomas came to the edge of the boat, holding out a hand, and she took it and climbed aboard.

"I've got the boat ready, and will cast off," he murmured before swooping in for a gentle kiss.

The last few days they'd settled into their 'coupleness', and she welcomed every tiny caress and kiss. Now, if only she could get him to ask her again. But time didn't wait, and they'd already put off heading out with the trawler, because Cherie had been insistent that she needed to give Kelly an all-clear before she'd categorically allow Kelly to captain the vessel.

Sliding her bum onto the seat in the wheelhouse, Kelly looked down at the discarded sweet wrapper. "It's all your fault, old friend," she muttered. "No more sweets for me."

The engine started smoothly, and after checking to make sure that Thomas had the ropes coiled on the deck and was ready, she guided the trawler slowly toward the open water.

Turning on the fish finder, she started scanning, remembering her father's words to 'look for a good-sized shoal, but only take what you need.' The words had an extra importance these days, with the major and his people flying in yesterday. Choppers now filled the sky over the island as they ferried the staff from the distant ships. Now with the US ships Brittin, Comfort, and Tortuga on standby off the coast, she felt once again easy about their situation.

Their own people continued the patrols along the channel separating mainland from island. Another ten zombies had been discovered and dealt with. Just yesterday, with the major onboard, their people had highlighted the situation, dealing with the incursion.

Today, the aim was to restock the shop with seafood, since it had been six days since she'd last worked. Seafood had come to represent a large portion of the resident's diet, which Cherie called an 'overwhelming triumph.'

Kelly wasn't quite sure she necessarily agreed and privately hoped that someone from the mainland might be found who'd assist with the fishing duties. The last few days she'd spent with Thomas had reinforced that she really didn't want to do this for the rest of her life.

She spied a shoal on the radar and gave the order to deploy the nets. She carefully guided the vessel forward so they'd capture enough fish to fill the smaller hold. More than that and she'd flood the market. Not an outcome she really desired.

Hours passed. They brought the fish net in and had finished sorting and clearing, then climbed back to the wheelhouse when she caught sight of a vast bobbing area of debris coming in her direction.

She peered closer, grabbed the binoculars to check, then swore. "Thomas? Thomas, get up here!" If her mind wasn't playing tricks, then they had a very large issue, because there had to be at least fifty bobbing zombies, clutching logs and other floating matter.

He stepped in and caught sight of her gaze. "What?"

She pointed. "Out there. We need to move. Get back to the mainland and get the men out here. Pronto."

He took the binoculars from her hand. "How many?"

She shrugged as she fired the engines. "Have Dan hold on, this is going to be rough and quick."

Thomas opened the door, called to Dan to get up to the wheelhouse, now, then returned to Kelly's side.

"What?" Dan breathed, panting heavily.

"Shut the door and strap up," she instructed and glanced again at the oncoming force. "Shit. They're nearly on us."

The boat moved, surging against the tide, but it was slow, a monstrous beast weighed down, and Kelly's nerves wound tight as the first of the zombies came close to the hull.

"Fuck," she whispered. "Thomas?"

He had a small pistol in his hands and was already loading bullets into the chamber. "They won't get on board, Kel. I promise."

Her guts twisted as the boat continued the laborious movements while the swarm surrounded them.

Thomas moved and opened the door to the wheelhouse before she could yell at him not to. Then he was gone.

Fright chilled her, but she had to get them out of there, otherwise the zombies would pile on board. If that happened, they'd have no chance.

Tears coursed down her cheeks as Dan rocked and prayed in the seat beside her.

***

Thomas cut all extraneous thoughts from his mind, knowing the danger of these zombies. They weren't the weak variety. He'd noted the musculature and had seen them in action. Aboard the boat they were even more dangerous.

The roar of one as it clambered onto the deck should have stopped him in his tracks, but instead he looked for a secure location to shoot from. The zombie was advancing, its steps slow and steady, eyes gleaming with hunger, and a lesser man may have cowered.

With Kelly very much at the forefront of his mind, he advanced, weighing up the options while remaining aware that he didn't want to get caught between this bugger and another.

A roar behind him echoed, and Thomas turned to see another sliding over the side. "Fuck."

He needed them close enough to be assured of a killing shot. He'd only have one go. But he also needed to stay out of reach. Stepping back, he slid up the first step leading to the cockpit. Knowing retreat wasn't really an option but needing the incentive of being close enough for them to continue their advance.

Another step, and his foot slipped. "Shit!"

With his free hand, he clung to the railing and pulled himself up. The zombie was only mere feet away now, and Thomas aimed. The gun fired but glanced off the creature's shoulder. The second crowded in and a third was advancing. With only five shots left, he'd have to make them count.

He sighted and squeezed, keeping the pistol trained on the creature. It flailed and a trail of red exploded behind its head. "Thank God."

Without time to do any more, he aimed at the second, and the shot was true.

One left. In its eyes he read a cunning he'd not seen before, and it lurched to the side as Thomas raised the pistol.

It slipped in gore the other two had left behind and dropped hard to the deck with a growl. With bony fingers, it advanced, crawling along the wood planking. Thomas swallowed, sweat sliding down his forehead. Three shots left. What if he missed? Teeth gnashed as the stench of putrification filled the air.

The shot was true, but again the zombie moved, so that a furrow opened the skin at the creature's cheek, exposing bone and greenish, rotting flesh. Black-red blood flowed freely, and its jaw hung from tendons stretched tight.

The guttural tones of fury filled the air. This time Thomas aimed for an eye, hoping and praying that as the zombie was now almost close enough to grab his ankle, it would surely destroy the brain.

The shot squeezed out.

Micro-seconds passed.

Thomas held his breath.

The creature jerked and fell backward, the job complete.

Thomas slumped, holding the metal rail as if his life depended on it. He breathed in and out, before rising and turning, making his way back to the wheelhouse.

"You okay?" Kelly asked, holding out a hand.

"Yeah, but it was close run. There's three big buggers on the deck though."

"At least we survived, but with that many, we have to head them off before they get to the island," Kelly reminded him.

"Hmm," was all he grunted in return, his mind twisting and turning, trying to strategize while adrenaline continued to course through his body.

"What if we don't…?" Dan asked, eyes large and round with terror.

"The army guys are our last line of defence," murmured Kelly as she tacked the boat, heading in toward the main jetty.

Now the only noise cutting through the silence was the chugging of the boat's engines and the intermittent cry of a seabird flying overhead.

As they rounded the coastline, coming past the area where Jack and Addie's house was located, she pulled the lever to sound the whistle on the boat, using the traditional morse code call of three short, three long, and a further three short calls. "That should get some attention," she muttered before repeating the process.

An outline ran down to the water's edge. Who it was, Thomas couldn't tell, but it didn't matter. He opened a window and yelled, "Get Jack to meet us at the jetty."

The figure pantomimed not understanding. "Jack. Get. Jack!" he bellowed. They stopped, waved a hand, then sprinted back up toward the road and out of sight. "Keep signalling," he told Kelly, because he couldn't be sure whoever it was really understood.

The squelch of a signal came through the radio. "Wha…?" Kelly grabbed the handset. "Malina Bay," she called.

"Major McDougall here. What's going on?"

"Zombie forces in the water. I'm guessing about fifty or so. We have several corpses on board, but there's more coming."

Thomas held out his hand, and Kelly handed over the handset. "Major, this is Thomas. I need my people on boats now."

"We can wait for them to arrive," the major answered.

"With all due respect, major. They aren't clumped together on a single piece of debris. They're all riding their own, and three changed directions to head toward us. We run the risk of them splitting up before they arrive, and there's too many places they can hunker down and hide. We need to try to stop them before they reach the island."

Silence stretched. Thomas had the feeling the major would attempt to overrule him. Even though their agreement clearly said that in these situations his people were the first line of defence, a man like the major wasn't used to giving up control.

"Fine," he finally said. "Your people go out and do what they can. Mine will begin patrols of the beaches."

"In teams of two?" Thomas asked.

"Yes." There was a definite bite to the answer, but Thomas simply grunted as the connection broke.

Dan and Thomas hurried from the wheelhouse. "We need to fasten alongside, then you make sure the boat is emptied and cleaned after the unloading team come collect the fish. Kel and I are going to catch a lift back to the house and collect the South Bay and head in the direction they were travelling."

Dan nodded, and together they worked with speed. "Why?"

"Because I need something faster and more manoeuvrable. And I don't have enough fuel in this anyway," Kelly answered. "Get the mechanics in to give her a good look over," she added.

Jack arrived. "What the fuck? The major said there's an invasion!"

Kelly joined them as Thomas climbed off the boat, and they moved along the jetty to another boat. "About fifty that we saw," answered Kelly.

Two service people jogged up. "The major said you've got carcasses."

"On the boat," Kelly called. "Feel free to take them away."

The two nodded before heading down to Dan.

"Fuck," Jack muttered. "You need to get to Kel's house."

They jumped into Jack's car, and he drove carefully but fast, pulling up at her house mere moments later. "Thanks," Tom called as they jogged toward the boat. By agreement, the key had been left in the ignition, so she didn't need to track it down.

Once on the boat, Tom unhooked the ropes and Kelly started the engine. "It's going to be rough, hold on," she called, and the boat lurched forward.

They saw other boats heading out too. Kelly opened the throttle and the boat surged forward, eating the distance between them and the teams, then slowed so they kept speed with the other boats.

Thanks to Jack, they now had a handheld loudspeaker on board, and Thomas lifted it and pressed the button. "Don't get too close. They've worked out how to climb aboard, so don't take chances. Aim for the head, because we know that works, and remember, we can't afford for them to make landfall. Try and stick together, but if you catch sight of runners, stay in groups of two."

Heads nodded, and once he was sure everyone understood, they moved, with Kelly and Thomas taking point, and he noted that the group had now dispersed into a long, wide front. During the initial planning phase, Thomas had taken time to explain that due to the speed of the South Bay they could circumnavigate any attack, so they tacked wide, heading to the furthest extreme of the group, hoping to herd them back toward the centre. But the further they travelled, the more they saw in the distance.

"Another group?" Kelly muttered.

"Could be. We should try and pull them closer to our existing group." Privately he wasn't sure this would do the job, but what other option did they have? "Let's see what we can achieve."

He reached into the lockbox they'd mounted on the shelf at the front and pulled out the pistol and started loading bullets into the chamber. Six, he counted, ensuring he could access others swiftly should they need to.

The boat zoomed along the surface of the water, and as they drew closer, he saw these zombies were smaller, less muscled. "We need to get to that outer edge," he said as he indicated where the last members of the zombie infestation swam.

"Look," called Kelly. "Sharks."

He noted the fins rising from the surface. They didn't know if sharks would attack but knew very large great whites swam this area. Alpha predators, and the zombies were in their environment. "Let's see who wins the battle between them."

Kelly nodded. "Close your box and hold tight."

He followed her instructions and just in time grabbed the bar in front of him as she turned wildly, creating a wave. It undulated, forming a foaming top which crashed down, sending several zombies off whatever they clung to and into the water. They disappeared below the waves.

Those left clung tight, growling with menacing intent, but Kelly shook her head at them and muttered while Thomas watched them float ever closer to the first knot of zombies.

"Do it again," he instructed, and Kelly hauled on the wheel, reefing it, and the boat turned. Changing her angle, Kelly created another wash, shoving more below the surface.

Now the sharks moved in, their fins cutting through the wildly disrupted water, and grey, red liquid stained the water around them. Kelly slowed the boat, and in silence, they watched the churning of the water.

"Do you think...?" Her voice croaked.

"I don't know. I mean, do zombies even breathe?" he muttered.

"Oh fuck! Thomas, what if they don't?"

"Then they'll work that out soon, and we'll be in real danger."

Her hand clasped his. Tight. For a second, he drew comfort from the touch, before disengaging.

"We have to see if we can get the rest over to the first batch," he said.

She returned to the captain's seat, and he settled himself in, fastened the seatbelt, and opened the lockbox.

"We do one more round, then we start eliminating," he instructed.

Kelly nodded, and though he knew she was terrified, she followed his directions, moving closer this time so the wave would be unpredictable. The creatures growled, but the tactic did its job, dragging more under the surface of the water, while the number of fins grew larger.

Gripping the bar in front of him, he took aim and started picking them off. They couldn't move fast enough in the melee, and one by one, he counted six down. "Stop the boat while I reload," he yelled at Kelly, and she followed his instructions.

Knowing the barrel of the pistol was hot, he opened it nonetheless and slid six new bullets into the chamber. It closed with a snap, and he took a moment to prepare for the next attack, eyes closed and inhaling deeply. A roar sounded, and he snapped his eyes open and glanced back. A hand, or more correctly, a claw gripped the rear of the boat, nails biting deep into the fibreglass of the body.

"We've got company, Kel!"

She punched the throttle and the boat shot forward, but another hand snaked its way up. "Shit!"

Fury pumped in his veins, keeping a rapid tempo, but he wouldn't rush, otherwise, he'd miss. Not an option. Thomas waited until one misshapen head rose above the back of the boat and squeezed off a round. Ping! It missed, instead catching the casing of the boat's engine.

The zombie advanced, tugging itself over the back, rising up like some demonic creature.

His guts seized, but his hand never wavered. Whomp! The head exploded and the creature fell from the back of the boat, but the second had clawed its way up while he'd been concentrating on the first. Slithering a leg up. It started to rise to a crouch.

"Stop the boat," he screamed, and Kelly stilled the engine. The twin actions of that and the bullet sent the zombie flying into the water. "Throttle! Now!"

Kelly threw the boat forward again, and it responded with a splutter. "There's something wrong with the engine," she called.

He knew what it was as black and oily smoke puffed up into the air. "Get as near to shore as you can," called Thomas, clutching the loudspeaker in hand. At least now the other boats were within distance, and he pressed the button. "Zombies here!" He waited, watching for some sign that they'd heard him, then turned to Kelly. "Can we get nearer as we make for shore?" he asked her.

"I don't know. The engine's sluggish." She turned to look at him, and he read the whiteness of her features, the pinch around her lips. "I don't know if we'll make it, Thomas," she muttered. She killed the engine and climbed from the seat, and he followed suit.

"Fuck." One little bullet is all it took. Peering closer, Thomas saw the crack in the housing where the bullet had slammed through. His lack of aim had damaged their chances of surviving, and the sourness of bile coated his tongue.

He looked up, shading his eyes, and noted that one of the smaller craft cut away from the rest and zoomed in their direction. In moments they were almost close enough to touch, and the wash left the South Bay rocking in the swell.

"Hey, Thomas! Kelly! What the...?" The man's gaze took in the damaged engine. "You've got a problem there. Need me to tow you in?" He looked doubtful, and Thomas guessed he was sizing the situation to see if his own engine could carry the extra load.

Kelly shook her head. "You know we'd both be adrift soon enough if you attempted it. Get back to land, have Jack scare up someone with the Coast Guard vessel. It'll be able to tow us into shore."

"Okay, I'll go get help."

But when the man looked over his shoulder, Thomas knew what he saw. A number of zombies were drifting in their direction, and it took little imagination to see teeth gnashing and claws extending. He shivered, hoping to lose the sudden chill invading his bones.

"Be as fast as you can, I think I can hold them off for a little while," Thomas muttered. "Take Kelly with you though."

"Over my dead body," she countered, and catching sight of her, he noted the way her lip curled. "I have a pistol, and I can hold my own," she growled.

"Well, if you two are sure," the other boater clarified, though from the look on his face, Tom was sure he didn't think they'd make it.

"Go, and be fast," urged Kelly.

He left them, the wash sliding the boat up and down.

"Thomas?"

He turned, pulled Kelly close. "We'll get through this." *If only I could be sure we would.* But life came with few guarantees these days, and Thomas knew that while he'd give everything to ensure Kelly's survival, he just couldn't rely on hope and wishes. They were in a dead boat, in the middle of nowhere, alone. With zombies about to descend.

They settled into the seats, Kelly reaching into the bag for one of the water bottles she'd stashed before their last mission. He accepted it in silence, eyes watching for signs of attack.

"This isn't quite how I thought today would go," she whispered. "Today was supposed to be about gathering resources. Getting ready to hand over some of the responsibility for the day-to-day feeding of the island."

He reached out and grabbed her hand. "I know. So, now that we have time, what do you want to do once this is under control again?"

Inhaling, she scooted closer. "I want..." She cleared her throat. "I was talking with Addie the other day. Discussing babies."

His head turned in her direction. "Babies?"

She nodded. "I guess in the last few years, I stopped thinking about families, and what I really want from my future. Until we kind of..."

"Got back together?" he added.

"Something like that. I mean, now I've told you I want that ring," she said, and Thomas grinned at the emotions that swirled inside. Pleasure. Pride. Love. "I still do," she continued. "But I also want more. I want children and a home."

Thomas blinked. "You don't want to live in your parents' place?"

"I love the house, it's full of memories, but I felt isolated as a younger child. An only child. That changed once I met you and Jack, but I don't want that for my kid. For our kid."

Heat suffused him. He hadn't allowed himself to really consider how he'd feel when the time came to talk of babies and families. He'd fantasised about her pregnant, including recently, but the realities of planning or considerations of lifestyle hadn't entered the equation. At least, not until now.

"Okay. What about study?" he asked.

She screwed up her face. "I don't know. I mean, there's opportunities, and Australia's going to have a huge job sorting out the mess the country is in. There's lots to rebuild, not just the economy but also houses, office spaces. I'd like something to do with that, I think." While she talked, Kelly started sliding shells into the barrel of her Ruger LCRX pistol. It was smaller and sleek, while his was meaty, a more traditional Taurus M65 357 Magnum.

He took the box of shells she offered and slid another six into the chamber of his pistol. "Well, I guess, when this is done, we could maybe ask some questions. You want to go to university?"

She laughed now. "I always planned to, and yes, I think I'd really like to have the opportunity."

"Then we ask questions, once we sort this mess out. I doubt you're the only one but..." A small band of ravenous creatures came closer to the boat. He wondered if the sharks could be enticed, but discounted that. They'd likely still be busy with feeding on what they'd found in the water. "Kelly, once this is done, we head to my place. I need to find some stuff. Grab clothes..." You need to dig the ring out of the safe. Time's wasting, and you may find chances hard to come by.

"Should we strap in?" Kelly asked as the zombies came ever nearer.

"I think that's probably a good idea. Unclip the pin stopping the seats from spinning though, so we can move around."

She followed him down, finding the pins that were added when the boat was modified by its previous owner, then they both sprang back up into the seats and pulled the lap sashes into position with a snick.

"I love you, Kelly," he told her, hoping this wasn't the last opportunity they'd both have.

"I love you too, Tom. Always have." She grabbed his hand, squeezed, then released it.

A subtle lapping wave dragged three zombies still clinging to the debris closer.

CHAPTER 16

Kelly inhaled, the nerves melting away under the soft breeze. Thomas waited beside her, still and stiff. She knew they both understood the gravity of their position. Precarious didn't even begin to explain it. At least some of the boats have drifted closer; they might come to our aid.

The nearest zombie reached out to her, and she couldn't miss the smell of putrification. She squeezed off a shot and watched as the creature jerked, a tear opening along one rotting shoulder. It roared with displeasure or pain? She didn't know which, but to be honest, she didn't really care either. All she knew was their hands paddled them closer and posed a threat to their lives.

The eyes—orbs of streaky grey and milky white—distended as they reached out with a grasping hand. Bang! went Thomas' gun. The large pistol recoiling only slightly, unlike her much smaller offering.

The zombie fell back into the water and flailed. The others simply bypassed it, coming closer as the tide dragged the boat nearer to shore.

Once more Kelly aimed, and the bullet sliced through a spurting eye, and the second creature toppled into the water and down, without a whimper.

The third, a female this time, opened her mouth as Thomas' pistol erupted once more. The maw opened wide, and the creature dropped down onto the debris, suddenly still and silent.

Another flotilla was incoming, but a distance away.

"We should reload," Thomas grunted and they watched the boats come closer.

A sound rent the air, the whine of a larger vessel moving quickly. Kelly turned and smiled. "It's the Coast Guard vessel."

The creatures were moving faster now, arms reaching out as the large boat pulled alongside, a trim body sliding down the side with a heavy rope in hand. "We'll take you along behind us." The woman smiled then nodded in the direction of the incoming flotilla. "You need to deal with that?"

Kelly and Thomas picked this next batch off, and Kelly was very pleased to see that no more appeared to be drifting in their direction. "Looks like that's all of them."

The woman climbed into the back of the boat. "Nice looking vessel you have here. Jack said it's pretty fast."

Kelly nodded and explained what they used it for. "If we can move between the island and the mainland at speed, we should be able to outrun the zombies. It'll be more useful once we get these service guys on the ground."

"I see there's one or two who look good in uniform. Tom here too. He's pretty fine in those blues he wears."

Kelly clenched her fists. "He retired."

The woman stared at Thomas who was turning a beet colour. "Really?"

"Uh, Janet, how about we focus on the task?"

She laughed at Thomas' stiff remark. "Getting all hot under the collar." And she fanned herself.

"He's also taken," Kelly murmured, vainly attempting to hold onto her temper. The woman clearly couldn't read the vibes they were both putting out, Kelly thought, and that really rankled.

"Oh well. That's a shame. Lucky bugger, you." Janet hip-checked Kelly. "I always wondered how I'd entice him, but it seems I'm too late. So, back to the servicemen then." And she grinned.

***

Thomas waited until they were safely tied up at the marina, even though time was of the essence and Jack was pacing, his face tight. "Thank God. I'll get you back to Kelly's," he muttered as she came flying up the jetty.

"Not home. The trawler's tied up at the jetty. Take us there," Kelly ordered. "I'll get the mechanics to look at the motor, and I'm hoping we'll be back onboard in a few days. I doubt the casing will be an issue, because there's plenty of boats sitting around, and if necessary, we may have to gut one or two to fix it, but it shouldn't take long." She climbed into the backseat of the car. "Good thing you have your car and not Addie's."

"What the fuck happened out there?" Jack demanded.

Thomas sighed. "We found it wasn't just one incursion, but two. We need to get back out there, check and see if we've missed any."

The handheld set on Jack's belt squawked. "We've got incoming, Jack." Tam's voice scratched through the radio, and Thomas shivered, realising that some had made it through the boat teams. "The major and his people are heading out to comb the beaches and dispatch whatever might make it to land."

"Okay, I'm with Thomas and Kelly back at the jetty where her boat is moored. Have the major meet us here." He clicked off the speaker. "Take us out, we'll do a patrol all the way around the island and see who else is out there."

"Sure thing," Kelly answered.

Thomas wasn't sure that was quite the wisest option. "Have them send us a couple of guys with big guns to go out on the boat with us."

Kelly glanced at him with a question in her eyes, but he didn't speak another word until they were climbing aboard.

"What was all that about, Tom?" Kelly queried.

"Out there today? We came close to buying it, Kel. We need people with big guns, who can shoot straighter than I can."

Kelly slowly blinked. "You couldn't help hitting the motor. It was an accident."

"A foolish accident that nearly cost us our lives, Kel. And they're growing bolder. More people and more guns—"

"Armaments on a boat leads to more accidents," she countered, sliding a hand over his cheek. "Don't pile blame on yourself." She reached up and kissed him on the lips. "We get through this together."

He leaned his brow on hers, wondering where the strength of this woman came from.

"Okay, kids. Kissy-face time later. The major and his men will be here in five," interrupted Jack.

They didn't spring apart, and Thomas would have stayed longer except Kelly murmured she needed them to get the boat ready. The tide had changed, and she'd need to get them out of here quickly, at the rate things were going.

When the major and his three men arrived moments later, each carrying a large munitions box, Thomas urged them aboard the vessel, then he and Jack cast off the ropes and secured them.

"Major, you might like to head up those stairs," Thomas muttered, noting that no trace of the earlier interruptions by zombies was apparent.

"I don't know how you guys have done it," muttered one of the armed personnel. "I mean, you're apparently doing well and thriving under extreme circumstances. I'm Adrian." The man held out a hand. Thomas took it and shook. "And these are Mark and Luca. We're all crack shots, which is why the major brought us."

The blond guy that Adrian had introduced as Luca shook his head. "We've had some interaction with the zombies, but you guys have been dealing with it since day one. The major said there's significant changes?"

"Evolution," muttered Jack, and Mark's eyes widened.

"We've noticed changes in their body structure, their speed, and the fact that they're learning," Thomas added.

"Learning?" Mark repeated. "Like how?"

Tom squinted in the late afternoon glare. "Like how to swim, or at least use debris like a bodyboard to cross the water. Shark-infested water."

"Well, fuck me," Luca muttered, sliding his hand through his hair.

They settled in under the cover of the wheelhouse, looking out at the water.

"Thomas?" Kelly called as he was clambering up the steps.

"What's wrong?" he asked as he launched through the door.

"Oh, uh, describe to the major what happened. He wants details, and I need to concentrate as we round Rocky Point." Many a ship, large or small, had run aground, with a narrow channel only to traverse through this area.

The Malina Bay fought its way through the waves, and while he watched Kelly's tacking, it wasn't until they were through the rocky zone that he once again breathed freely.

"She's a hell of a captain," muttered the major.

"That she is."

"You're a lucky man. If I were single and a few years younger, I might have considered her fair game."

"I'm no one's game, major," she told him, and Thomas smiled at the bite in her tone. No, Kelly is very much her own person.

"The situation is we found two separate incursions of zombies. No humans though, but that doesn't mean they aren't out there, watching and waiting. The zombies were using the debris to cross the water on. We managed to deal with some, but the teams were unable to get them all."

"They got back and said there were a few they missed, but the water was too rough to continue," the major explained.

"Every man in charge of one of those boats is well trained," Kelly offered.

"They all made it back safely?" He should have asked, but the concern for Kelly's safety had taken centre stage.

"Yes. Your man took the headcount himself, but was very relieved to hear you were under tow as I was apprised. What happened?"

"An attack, then a stray bullet in the engine," Thomas said.

"I see. And the boat?"

Thomas inclined his head at the major's question.

"Already under repair. Our repairmen are gutting other smaller vessels to make the necessary repairs, and she'll be back in service in a few days," Kelly answered.

"You're all very capable on this island," the major said, his grin lopsided. "You've got a good life, and you've negotiated a number of concessions which are beneficial to your lifestyle going forward. I'm retiring next year and may be looking for—"

Thomas didn't need to wonder at the major's suggestion. "Life is pretty good. We've got housing and fresh food. There's a school for the kids of primary age, and we'll be looking for high school teachers soon, to reopen the upper grades."

"And a fully stocked and serviced hospital too," Kelly added. "What does your wife do?"

The major smiled. "She's an architect."

Now Thomas smiled. "Well, we may be able to do you a deal," he answered, and glanced at Kelly.

"Ahead," whispered Kelly, and in front of them was a zombie, clinging to a piece of shipping, half-slid off into the water. "That's what we came across."

It looked up and bared its teeth. The major took the offered binoculars from Kelly. "Well, it seems the new task is to stop them from getting to the beaches in the first place. We'll need to report back what we've seen to mission command in Canberra. In the meantime," he said as he laid aside the binoculars, "can the men get to the front of this ship?"

Kelly explained how to access the front hatch and slowed the boat as the major stepped out of the wheelhouse and relayed his instructions to Luca.

Moments later the man clambered out the front, using the hatch opening to hold him in place as the boat dipped and swayed. The zombie was only several meters in front when Luca raised his rifle. Bam! The ricochet echoed, but the zombie was gone.

Kelly took up the binoculars and Thomas watched her. "I think that's it for here, major," she muttered and gesticulated for Luca to return. "Thomas, can you..."

"I'll go down and check the hatch," he said and scrambled to complete the task, then returned. "All secured, Kel."

Sliding the handle of the throttle to open, the boat chugged on again. "She's not the largest ship, but she does the job. Dad bought her new thirteen years ago and trained me in every aspect. I can strip down the motor to make repairs, not that I want to. I can run any piece of equipment. The only external electrical addition he allowed was this," she said as she pointed to the fish finder.

"Amazing. And you intend to continue once things settle?" the major queried.

"No. Not exactly. I'd like to go to university and study. I finished school and there were some things that happened." Kelly glanced in Tom's direction. "But I think, in the end, things worked out the way they were meant to."

"That's a very strange view of the world," he commented as Thomas came up behind Kelly's seat and slid a hand on her shoulder.

"My view of the world has changed in the last couple of years, major. Once you've been here a while, yours may too."

In the hours that followed, as darkness settled, the wheelhouse became silent, apart from the motors, until finally, they tied up at Kelly's jetty.

Thomas offered to take them into town while Kelly prepared a meal. After they left the house, the large men squeezed into his vehicle, the major turned to Jack. "You've got excellent men and women. I've been meeting with them, as you suggested, and while I have some further suggestions, I see and agree with the thinking behind your requests. I've also asked for volunteers to come immediately from home."

Jack harrumphed. "Like what positions?"

"Several middle and high school teachers. Science, maths, and technology, along with English. Also, an oncologist, at the urging of our medical staff, and a paediatrician, given the number of younger children on the island. You only have one veterinarian, and she's severely overworked, so we're looking for one of those too. Your sergeant of police requested a judge. I think it would be best if we see what's on the ground here first though."

"We need more fishers. Kelly doesn't want to do this forever, not that she wants to relinquish the boat, but I think she'd be open to leasing it," Tom explained.

Jack frowned. "I didn't realise—"

"No," Thomas said before Jack could open a conversation he had no intention of having in front of the major.

They'd reached the outskirts of town when a flash of white, scuttling across the road, caught his attention. "Holy fuck, they survived!"

CHAPTER 17

Kelly was making her way over the hillock, the men trailing behind her, carrying the last few fish they'd collected on the way back to land. Though she ate fish regularly, catching a few beautiful, fleshy snapper would make dinner a breeze, she thought.

"Come on," she told Luca and Mark who'd been salivating over the fish. "These fish need cleaning before you take them back for your mates."

One snickered. "Mates," he said with a thick mid-west American accent.

She opened her mouth to speak again when suddenly she heard the sound that always froze her guts. The grinding moan of a zombie on the prowl.

The sound stopped her in her tracks. She turned to the men following, raised a finger to her lips, then turned back, peering into the gloom.

Where is it? She took a step beyond the dune and into the open. The growl came again, and she turned, saw it behind Luca. "Watch out!" she screamed and scrambled backward.

Mark and Luca turned, raising their rifles as the creature swiped out with a meaty claw. Blood spurted and Luca stumbled.

Mark remained still, like a statue.

"Run!" Kelly screamed.

Everything moved in slow motion, like a bad movie running on a screen. Blood pumped in her veins, but her mind equated action to pushing through a rice pudding. The fish dropped to the ground.

She grabbed Mark's gun, his hands relinquishing it to her as she cocked it and fired.

The creature jerked and turned, advancing on her.

"Fuck!" She scrambled back, needing to put distance between her and it, more than aware of the damage those claws could do.

With the added advantage of knowing the terrain, she shuffled down the dune and pelted toward the house, then redirected herself. She'd need to open doors, and that would give it time to catch up. They moved fast. Her brain whirred. Where to?

Dithering about cost seconds, then the idea came. The brush was heavy with dropped limbs. Uneven. If she could make her way, it would slow the creature down. She'd just need to be careful.

Legs pumped as she raced into the brushy scrub between her and the township. If she gave Mark time to carry out first aid on Luca, surely then he'd be able to come to her aid?

She crunched into the darkness. How well can they see in the dark? God, she hoped they were night-blind! Her chest bellowed with exertion as she ran, hoping to God she'd get out of this alive.

***

Thomas cursed as they swerved to miss the hulking zombie standing in the middle of the road. Its roar filled the cabin of the car. Thomas slid his hand into his holster then wound down the window. "Drive past it, Jack," he called.

"What the...?"

The major slid to the passenger side, and Thomas heard the rear window dropping. "We can shoot it as we pass," the major suggested.

Jack looked at him. "That side is civilian houses."

"So, pass it, turn, and come back. If we don't stop it, the cycle starts again, Jack," the major answered, with eyes on the creature.

Jack accelerated so they were past, then wildly swung the vehicle into a U-turn. Shoving his hand down the side of the seat, Thomas held on, but they were thrown about like toys. The car lurched from one side to another, and for a second, Thomas was sure they'd roll it.

They moved, counterbalancing, until the car was once more on its wheels. "Geez," muttered Thomas as he waited for the car to move again.

The zombie had started to advance, no doubt seeing an opportunity for prey. Thomas and the major prepared themselves, and as they passed it by, they squeezed their triggers.

The creature jerked once, then again as the bullets pierced flesh.

It wavered. Then crashed down onto the asphalt.

"Come about again," called Thomas, and Jack stopped the car, turned it this time in a controlled manner. He stilled the car metres away, and Thomas and the major piled out, Jack staying in the car.

"I'll keep it running, just in case," Jack called.

Slowly, the two men advanced. The creature on the ground groaned, and without another word, they both pumped bullets into the head. It exploded in a mass.

"Well, one less," muttered the major.

"We should be quick," Thomas urged the man away. "When you get back to base, organise a crew to deliver the remains to the crematorium."

They made their way back to the car, and Jack was already scaring up someone to deal with the guarding and clean-up after the corpse was removed.

Settling back into the car, the rest of the ride was silent. A sense of foreboding wrapped itself around Thomas, and by the time they'd dropped off the major, he was bouncing his knee up and down on the spot.

"It'll be fine. I'll pick up the others and drop them off, and you can settle in with Kelly," Jack offered.

If only life were that simple. If there was one... "I need to get back, make sure she's okay."

"There's only one," pointed out Jack.

"But what if there are others? We aren't safe anymore. Now that they know how to swim, there's only one way to deal with this issue. We must exterminate them." Slumped in his seat, Thomas focused on the road. "Never thought those words would pass my lips until the last two years, Jack. Live and let live. That was how I lived my life. I did my job, protecting people from criminals and danger, but the reasons and actions were clear. Now...?" He shrugged.

"It's hard, Thomas. Until now, it was just you. When you fall for someone... When you become one of a unit, your outlook changes. Look at Addie and I. Beforehand, I had no real plans to marry and have children. Now I have three and a wife. Protecting the future is my priority."

Thomas sighed. "It was always easy before. Now, until I know she's safe, I'm—"

"Terrified. I want to get home to Addie and the kids. Make sure they're safe too. It's a hard balancing act, juggling the two sides of who we are, Tom."

The road curved and they followed it, passing the underbrush which was dark and shadowed. The car swept forward until the house came into view.

His heart stopped.

In the driveway two men waited. One sitting on the gravel, leaning heavily against the car. His uniform torn and bloodied. The other standing guard.

The car had barely stopped when Thomas rushed from the vehicle. "Where's Kelly?"

Luca, his hand pushed hard against his belly, wheezed, "She went through the trees. Drawing it off."

Terror, an unwelcome rush of cold through his body, swamped him. "Fuck!"

He looked at the tree line. "Which way? Jack, stay here." He turned to Mark. "You, come with me, and if anything happens to her, I'll fucking kill you."

Why hadn't the soldier drawn off the zombie? Why let a woman, no matter how capable, face the danger alone? The words ran through his brain like an unwelcome recording.

***

Kelly's side hurt, and the tug of discomfort didn't ease even though she pushed a hand against the fleshy part above her hip. Gotta keep going. Draw him away. After the initial burst of speed, though, she'd slowed down, and the sound of shuffling was definitely louder now.

She knew that the shoreline wasn't far away, but she'd be exposed and in full view. Getting into the water and swimming wasn't safe either, not now that the zombies had mastered that. No, there wasn't any other option but to stay in here and try to evade the creature. At least until help arrived.

She swallowed a gulp and surged on, missing the small vine creeping across in front of her as she brushed it aside, then her foot caught on the roots, and she tumbled down, landing heavily with an oomph.

A shockwave of pain radiated through her ankle.

Trying to rise, the pain overwhelmed her. Oh God! Was this the end? How she'd die? Controlling the whimper, she slid to the side, dragging her useless foot behind her.

The stomping sound of the zombie grew louder.

Tears stung her eyes, but she refused to shut them. If this was her end, she'd face it head-on.

***

Somewhere nearby, Thomas heard the creature lumbering. It didn't move with stealth, but with intent. His fingers itched while the holster bumped against his side. Jack, instead of Mark, was following, but fury and terror scorched Thomas and urged him to move swiftly.

It was too dark to see Kelly's tracks clearly, but the sounds pointed the direction effectively, and he followed, every frantic beat of his heart a reminder that he had to find her before the zombie did.

His guts ached, and sweat poured down his neck, a rivulet, as he dodged and weaved, moments ticking by so very slowly.

A crash echoed, and he realised he must have passed it by, the creature dodging off toward the beachside.

In the distance something cowered. Something large.

It shrank down further as he approached, then a limb crashed into him. "Fuck you," Kelly breathed.

"Kel?" he whispered.

"T... Thomas? Oh, thank God you found me before it did." She turned and moaned.

"You're hurt?" Terror once more ascended. "Have you been bitten?"

"No. But I think I've sprained my ankle."

The lumbering sounds stopped, then started again, growing louder. "It's coming this way. Can you walk?" He crouched down, scooping her up, and for a second, she clung.

"No. I tried, but the pain was too much and my ankle couldn't support me."

Jack careened into Thomas, and he turned, the primal need to protect his mate taking over. "Take Kel. I'll deal with the zombie," he growled.

She mewled as he must have jostled her. "Tom..."

He cupped her cheek, added a quick, hard kiss. "Be quiet and let me take care of this." He didn't think her incapable, but a sense of urgency was rising inside him.

Jack melted back into the underbrush as Thomas took up position. A bigger gun would have been more effective, but this one still had enough stopping power. He'd employ it again.

He waited, nostrils flaring, for the zombie stench to fill the air.

It lumbered into view. "Over here, asshole," he called, and the shambling mass before him lurched.

Sighting down the pistol, hand steady, Thomas exhaled and squeezed the trigger.

Time nearly stopped. Between one heartbeat and another the bullet zoomed through the air, then embedded itself between the eyes of the zombie.

The creature fell. Crashed with a thud, and Thomas stayed in position, suspended in that second. The zombie was still.

Slowly, Thomas lowered the pistol and turned.

Jack stepped forward and handed Kelly back to Thomas.

Kelly burrowed deep into his embrace and Thomas dropped his forehead down so he could inhale the scent of her. "God damn it, Kel, you nearly died," he muttered against her.

She trembled in his arms. "I had to help Luca. He was injured."

His Kelly, a warrior and protector. "Let's go home," he said, raising his head. "Thanks, Jack," he added.

Jack nodded his reply and together they headed back to Kelly's house.

As they reached the yard, he noted Luca still on the ground, but he appeared to be in a bad way, with blood smearing his shirt and pants, his face a stark white. Mark, with the mobile talkie device in hand, was crouched beside him, and when they came into view, he blanched. "Is… Is she okay?"

"I think it's a sprained ankle, but looking at Luca, I'm thinking he needs to get to the hospital straight away."

Mark ran his hand through his hair. "I was going to, but the keys are missing from the car."

Jack shoved his hand deep into his pockets. "Sorry. Can you lift him and keep pressure on the wound? Thomas, you take the back seat, and Kelly in the front. We can't elevate your foot, Kel. Sorry about that, but we'll get you help as soon as possible."

The group moved now, Jack unlocking the doors and assisting with lifting Luca into place. Thomas stripped off his shirt and passed it to them. "Use this as padding," he muttered.

Jack started the car and headed for the road.

CHAPTER 18

Kelly waited as they wheeled Luca into the emergency room. Thomas argued with Jack over something, and there was a distinctly mulish look on Thomas' face. Whatever they were arguing about, it appeared Thomas won, and Jack threw his hands into the air. She waited patiently in the vehicle as they both returned to the car, Jack getting in the driver's seat and Thomas in the back.

"What's wrong?" she asked Jack.

"Don't ask me, ask Lover Boy," muttered Jack. "I just want to get home and check on my own family." The engine growled to life.

"Two minutes, Jack. Swing past my house and we can do a car shuffle. I'll return yours in the morning, but Kelly's tired and hurting and it's better to stay here. Please," Thomas asked, and Jack muttered an imprecation.

"Fine. Whatever." They headed down the road in quiet, until they reached Tom's house and the men got out of the car.

Thomas caught Jack's keys as they careened toward him, and took the driver's seat. The car sputtered and Thomas looked down. "What the... You're almost empty."

Jack shook his head. "I was planning on fuelling in the morning, but with all the to-ing and fro-ing tonight it's got low. I do, however, keep a spare can in the back for emergencies." And already he was lifting the boot and pulling out a can before Kelly could blink.

After the task was completed, Jack told Thomas, "You'll need to make sure to fuel it up first thing."

Thomas grunted, both men headed to the house.

Kelly piped up. "We could drop Jack off and stay at your place tonight? The doctors will be busy with Luca, and I'll be fine until I see Cherie first thing in the morning."

Her ankle ached, but surely it was just a sprain. It would be improved, if not much better, by morning. Thomas could wrap it tonight and she'd keep it elevated. Not that she wanted to be in that house again, given the memories it evoked, but all she wanted now was to sleep, the energy that had propelled her through the evening wearing off. She felt like a limp noodle and probably looked worse.

Thomas looked at her. "You're sure?"

She nodded.

He sighed, and Jack grabbed his keys. "Yes, you'd best stay here. I'll see you both sometime tomorrow then he was gone.

Kelly turned to wave goodbye then cried out, pain arcing through the injured ankle which sh was sure wouldn't hold her up in that second, and Jack swung her up and marched her inside his home. It was a squat, block building, with carefully tended shrubbery at the front and a neat patch of plain lawn.

Thomas growled before digging in his pocket for keys. "Last chance. We can go home."

His words warmed the cold interior of her chest. I would rather be at home. She straightened up. "No. We're here, and I just want to get cleaned up and sleep. Tomorrow, I can worry about how I feel about being here."

The key turned easily, as Kelly held on, and Thomas opened the front door to his place then stepped inside.

"Oh..." The place was practically empty. Almost totally devoid of furniture. A single two-seater couch and a coffee table. The artworks she'd remembered long ago were missing, and instead, the walls were a plain cream colour. Beyond the dividing half-wall, the kitchen had only a small refrigerator and the ornate table and chairs she remembered had been replaced with an old, plastic table and three battered outdoor chairs. "Where's the furniture?"

"All gone," Thomas explained. "Mum got rid of a lot of stuff when Dad was sent to jail. Had to pay the legal bills and couldn't rely on the bank balance. Most of it was seized anyway."

He carried her through to the bathroom and settled her on the side of the bath. While he turned the shower on, she shucked her t-shirt and bra and noted he stripped down.

"Need help?" he asked.

Kelly nodded in answer to his question. The jeans were a snug fit, and if she could just get them and the panties down, she'd be able to shuck them. He crouched before her and carefully removed the shoe from her foot. "Oww," she murmured.

"Sorry. I'll be as careful as I can." But when he got to the sock he hissed. "You need to see a doctor, Kel. That doesn't look good at all."

He removed the sock, and she bit her lip, holding in any further protest, because she knew he was being careful. Then, like a stork on one leg, and holding him tight for balance, she shoved down the clothing before settling on the side of the bath, where he gently tugged the other leg off.

She needed a moment as nausea rose, and dropped her head down, inhaling deeply until it passed. "Tomorrow morning. Shower now, and you can strap it up tonight." She shrugged.

He didn't look convinced. "Kel..."

"A couple of pain killers and I'll go to bed. Honest. I won't do anything I shouldn't."

He sighed and lifted her back into his arms and stepped into the shower. The spray of the water helped a little, washing the grime of the terrible day away. She didn't ask about a brush for her hair until she was towelled off and settled in his bed with one of his t-shirts acting as a nightgown.

"Just wait here a moment," he muttered and left the room.

She heard the tap in the kitchen and sank back into the pillows that smelled like Thomas. He returned long moments later, the boxers he'd slipped into his only covering, and in the light, she noted the firm muscles of his chest. The sight was mesmerizing.

"Take these and drink this." Two small pills were followed by a glass of water, and she gratefully swallowed them as he slid an old-fashioned flat hairbrush onto the bedside table.

Kelly watched as he stalked to his cupboard, threw it open, and she laughed, the issue of her knotty hair forgotten. Just as he always had, clothes littered the bottom of the wardrobe. He'd never been one to fold and put away, and she distinctly remembered his complaints during the academy days that he had to keep his locker tidy.

"Nothing changes, huh?" she said.

He turned and blinked. "What?"

"Your wardrobe."

"Oh...yes, hah." He turned back, and Kelly lay back, closing her eyes. The throb of her ankle surely had to settle soon, right?

***

Thomas cursed himself for ten tons of foolishness. He should have put his foot down and demanded Kelly return to the hospital. Even now, her face was chalky, with bruises and lacerations from her wild dash through the bush evident. When his gaze travelled down to the haphazard strapping on her ankle, his throat swelled.

She nearly died out there. The tiny box in his hands felt like lead. *You should have given this to her years ago.* Now she lay in his bed, injured but alive. He wanted to ask, but he wondered if she'd say yes or no. What woman wanted to accept a proposal when feeling like crap? And he had no doubt she felt like that.

"Are you coming to bed?" she croaked.

"I..."

"Thomas? What's wrong?" She scooted up in bed, her gaze narrowed on the box. "Is that...?" Her face broke into a smile. "Is that my ring?"

He gulped. "Would you rather wait until—"

She laughed, the sound a tinkle of pure joy. "Wait? No way. Ask me now, Tom. Right here. Right now."

He wondered if he should get down on one knee then discarded the thought. She knew it was coming. Instead, he lowered himself onto the bed beside her, taking care not to jostle her. "Okay then. Kelly, I waited far too long to do this. I should have asked years ago. I love you. I think I did from the first time I saw you across the sports grounds at school all those years ago. I let my father get between us. Should have seen what he was doing, and I let you down."

She held up a hand. "I hope it gets better after this, but for the record? We were young, Tom. Too young, I think, to have made it work. We needed time to grow and be who we were meant to be. The universe gave us a second chance to sort out the mess, and we have. Along the way, we've learned a lot."

He laughed. "Always generous. Sometimes to a fault. But I should have asked, and I didn't. I'm not a fool though, I learned my lesson, and now, here, I'm asking you to marry me. To live with me for however long we have. Yes or no, Kel?"

"Yes," she whispered. "Now give me my ring."

And this time they both laughed as he fumbled with the box and pulled out the tiny, pale pink diamond he'd chosen for her so long ago. He slid the ring onto her finger and sealed the promise with a kiss.

CHAPTER 19

Kelly swiped at her neck, the sweat snaking its way down her
clothes and tracing a line along her spine. "I really hate these
recon missions," she muttered, changing the gear on the battered car
she drove.

"At least you know your way around here. I feel like we'll never get
the names of the streets and towns sorted," Luca whined.

She snorted. "Well, given this is our last mission, you'd better get it
sorted."

In the last three months she'd driven more miles than she had in
the last two years. She and Thomas had been guiding the major's
people around the towns they'd decided needed to be cleared before
any landing force could make inroads on the mainland.

Today he'd grandly announced that the first craft would launch in
the morning, the zombies from this region at least appeared to be
cleared. While the island would remain their main base for the region,
with the hospital services bolstered and communications re-engaged,
smaller encampments would be erected as they advanced inland.

Luca and Mark would both be part of the advance forces, and while
Kelly appreciated Luca's dry sense of humour—having spent part of

her recuperation assisting him after he'd been injured by the zombie—she was ready to move on.

Besides, she had one more test to take. One she hoped would prove positive. The small box waiting for her in the bathroom at home.

"Kel? Your crew satisfied with the intel?" Thomas' voice echoed over the wireless, and she couldn't stop herself from looking in the rear-view mirror where he bounced along in an old Toyota pickup behind her.

"Luca?" She turned toward him, and he smiled.

"We're all good."

Kelly relayed Luca's answer.

Turning off toward the jetty his men had barred off, she drove in silence. Tomorrow, she'd begin making plans for the wedding, though she had a sneaking suspicion Addie had already been hard at work, and had dragged Jessica in, given the girl remained an important part of their lives. Addie might be parenting three young children, and back at work, but she was a woman who took on missions with military precision.

The South Bay waited along with three smaller boats. Only these wouldn't follow back to the island.

"Well, Luca. It seems it's time for you to venture off on your own," Kelly said, turning off the ignition.

"I'll be back in a couple of weeks. Depends on how long it takes us to clear this zone, then some R and R. Maybe Mark and I will be cleared at the same time, and you can take us out on the Malina Bay."

Kelly shook her head. "No, Dan's taken over the lease on the vessel and the house. But I've still got the little runabout—we could go out on it. Do some fishing, then some beers on the beach. I've just got one or two stored away."

Luca grabbed her hands and shook them, his grip firm. "Yeah, that would be great. But I need to thank you. I'd never be back on active duty if you hadn't saved my ass that day. Thanks." Then he let her go and walked away. She watched him even as Thomas' arm snaked around her waist.

"All good?"

"Yeah. Let's head for home."

The two of them climbed into the boat, and she turned one last time, waved. "Think we've seen the last of the zombies?" she asked as they waited for the engine to kick.

"I hope so, love. I really do. Now let's go home and see if we can make a spark." He kissed her hard.

The trip was completed swiftly, and she was tying up at the main jetty within an hour. Hand in hand, they made their way up the street to the grand, old colonial house that had once been the mayor's residence. Since his death, it had sat empty, and now, after making the request through Jack and the other divisional leaders, they'd moved in. Most of their items were still in boxes, and Kelly wondered if they'd have some time, in between wedding prep and starting their new roles, to maybe set a couple of rooms up.

After they entered the front door, she turned. "Pour us both a cold drink, and I'll be out in a moment."

Scurrying to the bathroom, she reached into the drawer where she'd stashed the box and retrieved it.

The test kit looked like a long stick, and she quickly read the instructions before following them. One line started to appear, and she smiled. "Well, I guess that's the answer then."

Scooping it up, Kelly headed for the lounge, where he'd set out the drinks.

"So, what do we need to do first?"

She grinned and held out the plastic test kit, which he took. "Celebrate making a spark?"

His gaze dropped to the stick in his hands then back to her. "A spark?"

She nodded and he whooped, surged from the chair, and gathered her close. "Then we should celebrate." He stiffened. "Can we? Should we? Maybe you need to see the doctor first?"

She kissed him, hard, then pulled away. "No, I asked Addie's advice yesterday. She said so long as we aren't swinging off chandeliers, we should be fine."

His arms slid around her, gathering her tight against him. "Well then, let's get started, shall we?" Then he lifted her into his arms and strode toward the bedroom.

"I can walk," she said with a laugh.

"I know, but this is more fun," he muttered as he lowered her to her feet, their bodies brushing against each other.

"Oh? Oh yes." A little bit of devilry bloomed inside her mind. She stepped back and blinked. "It's a bit hot in here. Do you think we should lose some clothes and cool down?"

She slid her hands under the hem of her t-shirt and removed it in the time it took for him to shuck his. From there clothes hit the deck with speed until they were both naked, clutching each other on the bed.

Her legs parted, and he settled himself, his cock hard and ready while his fingers delved deep, seeking the hot warmth inside her. "Very ready, indeed," he muttered and withdrew his fingers.

Her nipples swelled, demanding his attention as he nudged himself into position.

"Such lush breasts. Hard and pink. Ready for me."

Thomas slipped inside her body, and she gasped, sensations rippling as he moved. "I... Oh God, Thomas. Don't..." She swallowed. "Don't stop."

He didn't. His hands roamed her body, tracing every dip and hollow before finally grasping her hips and holding her close.

Her body tightened, the vise in her belly shattering as she cried out.

He held her close until his orgasm, then he slumped. "I need...to get...off you. I'm too heavy."

"You're just fine. Stay," she whispered.

EPILOGUE

SIX MONTHS LATER

The plane touched down in Canberra, and as the representatives of the mid-coast Queensland region, Thomas and Jack stepped off the plane and onto the mobile steps, followed by their wives and children. Addie and her brood of three, two tottering, holding onto Luca's hands, followed by a very pregnant Kelly.

Thomas was there to assist her down the steps. "Watch your step, my love."

Waiting on the tarmac were the representatives of the Canberra region: Elaine and Liam and Dove with his wife Leonie.

In the months since the army had stepped in and begun taking control of the zombie issue, informal elections had been held. Regions banding together and forming steering groups. Eventually that had morphed into a government. Tomorrow would be the first sitting day of the newly reinstated Federal Government of Australia. As each region's representatives arrived, they were being met and ferried to varied communities within the area. Thomas and Jack had drawn the plumb position of the Farm.

"Hi, you must be Jack and Thomas. We're so pleased to see you," Elaine enthused.

Kelly had seen Elaine's picture, along with all the other representatives and partners, in the briefing pack in the folder of her backpack.

"Welcome to Canberra. Oh my, you look just about done it." She reached a hand out to Kelly. "Let's get you all settled in the vehicle, shall we?" As they settled in the small bus, Elaine moved into the centre. "So, we'll be travelling through the heart of Canberra on the way home. This way, you'll be able to see how much we've got cleaned up. This time you'll be staying with us, but the hotels locally have all been reclaimed, and we've made arrangements for a couple to be refurbed into apartments. And seeing there'll be families involved with you, we'll ensure they have adequate space for growing families."

Liam placed a hand on his wife's shoulder. "We've got representatives flying in today, and tomorrow morning at nine we'll be meeting at the old government house to take our oaths. Then we'll be in a position to meet in the great hall, where we will conduct the process of standing for positions, the vote, then meeting with the media."

In the last two months, radio and television stations had once again begun broadcasting. Newspapers were proving a little more difficult with supply chain issues, but Kelly was sure they too would be reinstated soon.

As the bus chugged toward Parliament House, she looked through the window. The flag flew high over the building, and for the first time, she knew the worst had passed. Australia would emerge from its cocoon in the very near future. A nation stronger than before, refined in a battle no one could foresee, populated with people who'd navigated the difficult times and were looking forward to the opportunities that lay ahead. Men like Thomas and Jack and the strong women like Kelly and Addie who walked alongside them.

The End
Or is it?

THE CELTIC CUPID TRILOGY

When Cupid—otherwise known as Diocail— is banished from his home on a remote Scottish Island, he's set a series of tasks by the great god Lugh, who also happens to be his father.

In **Blame The Wine**, he must bring two lovers together... BBW Cara and James, the man she's lusted over from afar who happens to be a super geek and head Veha Industries.

In **A Stranger's Embrace**, Diocail is driven to help an emotionally fragile Jane and Davis, a famous author. The task is more complicated, with the existence of Carstairs her could-be ex-husband and teenage daughter, Frannie.

In **Revenge on Cupid**, Diocail must take the ultimate chance and find his own happily ever after with Simone. Sometimes the past gets in the way and HEA's don't come cheap though.

The dusty, dingy little diner was full, even with its current state of cleanliness—or lack thereof. People from the surrounding offices didn't care about anything except the incredible, well-prepared food at a reasonable cost. They flooded in, like waves to the shore. As one tide left, another swept in.

"Honestly, Simone. I'm going to try getting his attention one more time. If that doesn't work, I'm out of there. I mean, how long can I keep trying?" Cara picked at the caramel tart she hadn't been able to resist with the cheap metal fork and flicked the blob of fresh cream that sat on top to the side of the plate.

"You've said that tons of times before. Besides, what are you going to do to get his attention? Hmm? Walk naked through the typing pool?" Simone bobbed the straw in her smoothie as she eyed her friend with a frown. "It's been what? Eighteen months since you saw him, and you've mooned over him from a distance ever since you met him. You need to move on, Cara. That is, unless there's something you haven't shared?"

The query was arch. Cara shivered even as she shook her head. "No."

Simone quirked an eyebrow, obviously unconvinced with the answer. Cara let out a deep sigh of frustration. "There's a position...it's only temporary, for a PA reporting directly to him." She speared a forkful of tart, chewed quickly and swallowed, before continuing. "In his office, full-time for the period of the engagement. I saw the memo yesterday. I mean, I have the skills, right? I can type, answer phones, make coffee, file, greet people. What's more, I can probably do it better than all those size eights in the typing pool that Ms. Jackman seems to prefer." She nodded thoughtfully. "All I have to do is get past the ogre in Human Resources."

Simone stared at her, disbelief clear on her face. "Girl, I so remember that woman. If you think you can get past her, you're doing better than I ever did. That's why I left Veha Industries, remember? Maybe it's time to haul out your resumé and consider some other options. Look for something better." Simone shook her head and billows of her crimson hair swirled through the still air.

Cara understood Simone only had her best interests at heart. But this time she knew the outcome would be different. Hell, she could feel it in the air. The tingle of expectation.

"Cara, the HR ogre will hang you out for breakfast before she offers you anything like a position in that office. Remember her mantra? Good looks and good work make for a positive workplace!"

Simone didn't sugar-coat anything. It was another great reason for their long- term friendship. Honesty. But Cara didn't want to hear the truth in the statement. Even if it was exactly as her friend said.

Cara nodded quickly. "Yeah, I know, but if I don't try, then I won't know how close I can get to him, right? And the only way to catch his attention is to get past *her* and see him in person." Cara quaked a little at the information she needed to share. The favor she needed to ask. "Anyway, I tidied up my resumé and dropped the application into a memo envelope yesterday, so it's too late to back out now. I mean, fortune favors the brave. Doesn't it? If I don't snag an interview, I'm going to visit the career advisor across the street and register with them." She shrugged. "I'll look for temp work until something more long-term shows up. I can see what they have on offer and well...who knows? Maybe a job with the right boss is just waiting for me. But I'd rather this worked out, to be honest." Her voice trailed off into a whisper. "I really wish he would notice me."

Simone took a long slurp of her banana drink, and Cara noticed her questioning gaze even as she squirmed. Finally, Simone nodded. "It's your funeral. So anyway, you'd better show me this memo if you want me to be a referee for you. I'm guessing that's what you need, right? I'll have to know what I'm supposed to say about you before they ring."

Cara smiled. "Thanks, Simone. I knew I could count on you." She slipped a piece of paper out of her handbag and handed it over. "Sorry it's a bit creased. It was in the bottom of my bag, I stashed it so none of the others from the pool would see. You know how it is."

Available from Love Books Publishing
books2read.com/CelticCupid

Direct Autographed Copy
https://www.imogenenix.net/CelticCupid

STAR OF ISHTAR

Warriors of the Elector
Book One

The first time Elara laid eyes on Grayson was when he rescued her from the clutches of a madman and his scientists who were kidnapping humans and conducting horrific experiments on them. That was years ago. In spite of her attempts to deepen their relationship, they remained nothing more than close friends.Now Elara is a medic with the Admiralty, and she knows what she wants. It's been Grayson since the beginning. When Elara is stationed on the *Star of Ishtar*, she arrives with a plan to further her career. But this time her plan has an added bonus—to finally get her man.

Grayson's spent years fighting the connection between himself and Elara. He's certain it only exist because he saved her life. But his will is failing, and he fears he just might give in to temptation.

"I finally made it." Elara Sudonne watched as the hull of the *Star of Ishtar* loomed in the inky darkness. She clutched her hands tightly together as the shuttle approached the hulking battleship.

This would be her new home and first combat ST placement for the Earth Empire. She quaked inwardly with nerves but fought to keep her serene exterior. Previously her deployments had consisted solely of on-planet expeditions and in rehabilitation and dirtside facilities. When the chance had arisen to move to the battleship, she'd grabbed it with both hands.

The frigid air chilled her bones as she sat in her shuttle seat, but a trickle of sweat inched its way down her back under the fresh gray wool flight uniform. Little puffs of vapor escaped her mouth as she rubbed her arms. Nerves stretched tight, she looked through the small portal at the front of the vessel. She wanted to tug at the collar that somehow seemed to have grown tighter as the ship loomed ahead, but instead she firmed her mouth, straightened her spine, and concentrated on the future.

"So damned long." She'd been working toward this outcome since the day Grayson Myatt and Duvall McCord had saved her from her Ru'Edan captors. She was lucky, she'd survived the 'experimentation' of the Ru'Edan leader Crick Sur Banden's scientists. "And all I have to remind me are my scars." She didn't grin at her own joke.

The person seated behind her jostled but she ignored it, lost in her memories. On that day, so very long ago, the young Elara, fresh-faced and with idealistic views of the empire, was taken from the mall where she'd been shopping with friends, thrust into the back of a transport vehicle, and given to the Ru'Edan scientists to experiment on.

For days they'd worked on her and others, seeking an average pain threshold of humans, slicing her skin then noting reactions and how long it took to heal. They'd cut her arms, body, and even her face, and now she carried the extensive scarring of the exercise as a reminder to herself and others of what they were fighting for. Freedom. The freedom of Earth and its allied planets.

She'd never relinquished hope, it had been her constant companion as she fought against the all-consuming terror. Then they'd found her in that dirty, disused warehouse. They'd found others too, in various states of death and decay. The smells of despair had filled the air with a fetid ripeness that she'd never been able to forget.

Since that day she'd promised herself that she would pay the Ru'Edan back for what they'd done to her. What they'd taken from her. Over the years, she tempered and honed the rage while remaining adamant that she would see the final act played out. She couldn't physically fight, but she had learned about trauma, knew it and understood how it affected a person, and used it as a weapon.

The iron will forged through her experiences had fed her determination, and she'd applied herself to study, finishing in the top ten percent of her class. She entered the medical program at the academy, working hard to excel. Her family remained supportive if perplexed as to why she had chosen to keep reminding herself of what had happened.

The maw of the *Star of Ishtar* loomed closer, opening its cavernous mouth as she watched through the portal. She could hear the voices of the shuttle crew signaling their intention to enter and land, the tinny confirmation coming swiftly. She watched avidly while the shuttle maneuvered, imagining the invisible shields dropping to allow it entry.

Her hands twisted with fear and anger, but she tamped down her emotions. Anger never helped anyone. Staying strong, knowing your history, and ensuring it couldn't be repeated, they were the answers, she told herself firmly, pulling herself from the grip of a dark past so horrific she still saw it in her dreams. She pushed it away to the recesses of her mind and focused on what she was about to do.

A squark overhead, the usual mechanical sound that alerted all on board to a transmission by the captain, caught her attention. "Attention all passengers. We are entering the shuttle bay. Please ensure when you disembark you remove all personal items. Move beyond the white line and wait for your designation."

The lights of the bay flashed as they entered, and once again Elara marveled at how far humanity had moved since they had first walked the Earth. She saw the opening of the structure as the shuttle moved into the bay, inching forward slowly until it stopped its ponderous motion and began its descent to the floor. Something deep inside warmed even as the shuttle's environmental systems began to synchronize with the cooler temperature of the *Star of Ishtar*, and she felt a smile crawl its way over her face.

Elara breathed in deeply, inhaling the metallic-tasting, recycled air and welcoming the calmness that settled on her body. Her eyes closed as she filled her lungs. "I'm here." There was more than a little satisfaction in her tone, and she smiled. She slowly exhaled, finding that center of peace she relied on.

A loud thud and clank echoed as the deep drone split the air. The engines were powering down, and there she was, on one of the Earth Empire's Emeritus class battleships. She sat in her seat, waiting for the all clear from the captain, and once it sounded through the cabin, she rose, tugging at the webbing belt and disengaging it.

The small backpack beside her was all she carried as she made her way to the exit, not needing to duck as so many others did. She stepped through the door, her hands gripping the rail of the cold, metal stairs which connected to the side of the gray shuttle.

She clambered down them slowly, savoring the experience. The sting of the cold on her hands from the stairs, frigid from even their brief exposure to the blackness of space, made her flinch inwardly. The shuttle journey from the Admiralty's strategic base at Aenna to their current position had taken just over an hour, but the whole time it felt like her heart had been in her throat. Her mouth was dry as she followed the new recruits from the ship into the landing bay. She stopped, silently noting the slight mustiness of the air, the recycled quality easily recognizable. Everything, including the oxygen, needed recycling in space.

All around her people swarmed, either around the ships or into the dogleg line that now formed ahead of her. Someone had opened the baggage locker of the shuttle, and the sound of dropping bags hitting the plascrete floor echoed in the air. Another crewmember guided trolleys to the other side of the shuttle, pulling out boxes with important day-to-day items for the ship, including vaccines and plants. She watched briefly, all the while listening to the alien cacophony. Voices called in welcome to old crewmembers, while new ones watched, many goggle-eyed in the fresh uniforms of newly minted officers and crewmembers.

Her gaze flicked around quickly, taking in the sights, sounds, and smells, pungent with oils and grease; burning smells from the scorched plascrete and the press of sweaty or nervous bodies. She joined the line silently, tacking onto the end, and stayed at parade rest, knowing the welcoming voice would cut through the air soon enough. She felt somehow disconnected from the main throng. Perhaps the knowledge that this was the outcome she had worked for years to achieve set her apart. However, still, she felt so...distant from everything around her. She smiled secretly at the bout of whimsy.

"Attention!" The voice boomed out over the plascrete of the docking bay, and she snapped her body into position, noting the commander who had bellowed the words. Technically, she outranked most members aboard the *Star of Ishtar*, except for the command and leadership staff, but she knew all newcomers had to join the welcoming parade, regardless of rank.

Fleet Captain Elphin came into view, his tired features topped by salt-and-pepper gray hair, which highlighted his cool blue eyes. Elara also recognized a body prone to a little middle-aged thickness. Following behind him was his second-in-command, Duvall McCord. A young up-and-coming officer, his status as a fast-tracking officer heading toward his own command, with Elphin both his mentor and captain, had become almost legendary at the academy.

She looked closely at McCord, noting the dynamic drive of his actions and movements. Soon he would achieve a promotion to captain, and she rejoiced for her friend. She'd followed his career with interest and had to tamp down a smile as his eyes betrayed the shock of seeing her before settling into their flat command persona. So he hadn't been apprised of her deployment, she noted, and she had to restrain the tiny feeling of surprise and satisfaction. She filed that snippet of information away.

She caught sight of the man standing behind Duvall. Grayson Myatt. He'd made her heart beat faster for years. Tall and blond with a muscular build and a sexy, tight, little butt, he had pools of deep-blue eyes that had always made her think of forever. He had a growth of stubble on his chiseled jaw, and her fingers itched to touch his perfect lips. Yes, since the day he'd found her in that nasty warehouse tied down like a ragged animal, she'd worshipped him from afar.

Now she had her opportunity to tangle with him, hopefully much closer than any chance that had ever come her way before. With a sigh, she pulled her gaze back to the captain and forced herself to concentrate on his words. She couldn't afford to have her commanding officer angry due to her being distracted.

"Welcome to the *Star of Ishtar*. Most academy recruits want to join us because of what we represent, but on this ship, we only take the best of the best. So, if you made it here, you're the ones we wanted to take a look at. Getting here is only the first step. Staying here is harder to achieve. Our people are the best. Earn your place, and in return, we'll make you one of our crew—a member of the *Star of Ishtar*. Only the best and the brightest wear our uniform and badge. You'll be expected to perform to your absolute limit then give some more. We don't tolerate people who don't pull their weight. Do us proud and wear your uniform with pride." The captain looked out over the new members of his crew. His voice had echoed during his speech, and now it died away.

He scanned the faces before him, and she could almost read his thoughts. There were new security officers and a smattering of other crew. Some of them were young and impressionable, and she knew a few wouldn't make the cut as crewmembers. Others would carve out their place on the *Star of Ishtar* and move to better positions and placements, like she would: the new SurgiTech, a younger female, experienced but untried on board a ship. She smiled at that thought.

Some of those who stood with her would be replaced as they failed the exacting standards the captain set. She'd heard that he was a firm captain, fair but demanding. He'd have to be to command this ship. The Ishtar had well over five hundred at full capacity, and the captain could select their placements as his command staff saw fit from the many who applied to join the crew. She sensed his satisfaction with the choices in the relaxation of his body.

Abruptly, he turned to Duvall, breaking her study of him. "Get them to where they need to present themselves." His words echoed as he walked away. He had a purposeful stride. Quick but unhurried, like he knew where he was going and how to get there. A man who knew how to get what he wanted. Someone to respect and admire.

"My name is Commander Duvall McCord. I am your second-in-command, and my direct subordinate is Commander Grayson Myatt. While you are aboard the *Star of Ishtar* you will be required to fulfill your duties efficiently. As Captain Elphin said, do your job right and you will be one of ours, with all the benefits that come with being a crewmember of the *Star of Ishtar*."

He paused and eyeballed each of the newer recruits, those fresh from the academy. Many of them paled under his gaze, and she smiled inwardly. Even the older people in the line seemed to quake beneath his scowl. He'd always had that air of innate authority, even when barely out of the academy himself. She knew his methods and watched him make full use of the carefully practiced tone of presence.

"Each of you has been assigned. You will present yourselves to the chief of your section. Those details will be found in your orders. Commander Myatt has organized a team to escort you to your cabins. You will have approximately one hour to prepare. We've arranged for crewmembers to escort you to your superiors. Be ready to present for duty. Any issues, you will, of course, take up with your section commander. Should there be need to take any further action, you will see Commander Myatt. You should only see me if you are a command crewmember or as a point of discipline. I am not one for small talk, so if you present to me, have a very good reason."

He delivered the words slowly and deliberately, and Elara restrained a small smile on hearing at least one gulp from those in the line nearest her.

"We run a tight ship here. Discipline and commitment are the two key factors we look for beyond loyalty in our crew. You will from henceforth represent our ship everywhere, and we do not tolerate anything less than the best." He looked around once more, the stern demeanor he wore so well reinforcing the message. If she hadn't known him for so long, she too might have missed the hint of humor glinting in his eyes, the one many took for coldness.

Her legs ached, and she wanted to move and relieve the pressure on them, but she held herself still, waiting for the command to dismiss. She wouldn't let herself or him down now. Not after she'd worked so long to achieve this position.

As the new ST, she had no previous experience on ships. She had vast experience in the field, but Elara was aware that would count for little in the eyes of most of the crew. She didn't intend to signal a weakness to anyone and least of all on her first day aboard the *Star of Ishtar*. That thought held her still and controlled.

She had big shoes to fill after her predecessor, Jamieson, had retired, even though she knew she could fill the void he'd left behind. As a long-term member of the crew—over twenty years—his tenure on the *Star of Ishtar* had placed him aboard since its launch. Due to his experience in the heat of battle with the Ru'Edan he had made a name for himself as the coldest of cold in the hottest of situations. She hoped to emulate that herself and carve out her own place aboard the Ishtar, as its crew lovingly knew her.

Duvall and Grayson knew how much she wanted to prove herself. They just wouldn't have expected it here, on the Ishtar.

She watched Duvall study her, then, quickly turning on his heel, call to those assembled, "Dismissed."

Once they started to move away, she softened her stance, preparing to turn when the call came.

"Sudonne! A moment if you please."

Elara turned to face Duvall. "Commander?"

"Welcome to the *Star of Ishtar*, Elara. While I am surprised you're the new ST, Grayson and I are pleased you could join us. But how did you manage to pull it off? Keeping it quiet that you were the new ST?" he asked, his voice deep enough to make most women shiver with anticipation.

She smiled, thinking it was a shame she didn't have any feelings for him except sisterly attachment, but then again, given his lack of deep commitment to women, maybe it wasn't such a shame after all.

She understood what drove him. He wanted his own ship and to captain his own future. They'd spent many nights over wine or ale discussing his beliefs that commitment grounded a person. Inwardly, she shrugged. He'd make those calls for himself, though she was sure that one day he would come across someone who would make him consider his choices a little more thoroughly.

"I'm pleased to be here, Duvall. Having an uncle who happens to be an admiral, he was able to let Captain Elphin know that I wanted to surprise you. It's a small world in the Admiralty. Elphin already knew of me, so he okayed my placement. Once the powers knew there was no impediments to me joining the crew, it was fairly simple from there." She felt a small smile creep onto her face, then let it drop away. "What do you think Grayson thinks?"

"Ah, still chasing him, are you?" He grinned, his eyes twinkling. "I think he'll be pleased you're finally old enough and you're here." He looked her straight in the eye. "But you may just need to remind him of that particular fact." He motioned for her to go before him, barking out a deep laugh. "Come on, I'll show you to your cabin."

Available from Love Books Publishing
Available in Ebook via Books2Read

Direct Autographed Copy
https://www.imogenenix.net/Warriors1

THE BLOOD BRIDE BY IMOGENE NIX

Hope just wants to be an ordinary nestling. She went to college and escaped, but now she's back and there's a secret everyone is keeping from her.

Xavier is the new master of the nest, ready to welcome home the daughter of the house who he has never met. He's unprepared for the woman who steals his breath and enchants him.

Now Hope and Xavier must fight for lives and those of the innocents. After all, it is only by overcoming the rogues that they will have a chance of a timeless future together. But will it be in time?

PROLOGUE

As silence descended on the house, the shadows grew—dark grays and blacks that bled into each other. First one figure then another broke away, making a run toward the house. Silent as the grave, they moved swiftly over dew-slicked grass. Then they stopped still. Waiting. Not a movement betrayed them until a signal propelled them back into action and they started crawling upwards. The walls damp coating no barrier to the intruders that ascended in the darkness.

The sound of each window breaking shattered the quiet—the figures were inside. Screams echoed through the night. Yet, in this area of large estates, heavy with noise-absorbing shrubbery, no one could hear those within. The blood-curdling screams went on and on before finally dying away.

Just one sound echoed through the night: The sobbing of a child.

The front door opened and figures trooped out—ghostly specters against an inky night sky, broken by a single outline. A child in white, carried at the center of the pack.

No sound broke the silence as they moved toward the trees surrounded the house.

Flames now licked at the manor: A deathly glow of oily smoke rising.

All that remained was a single person—wrapped in a cape of midnight blue beyond the house—watching them melt away.

Jemima moved toward the burning structure, breaking into a run as she breached the threshold. Vainly she attempted to enter, but the heat drove her back.

Now dashing tears from her face, she raced across the graveled driveway toward the gates, where the guardhouse was located. No sign of life existed within the building and some instinct of survival slowed her pace to a careful creep. Out of breath and heaving from exertion, she nervously checked within.

Small puffs of white vapor colored the glass. She darted from one window to another. Her cloak drawn tightly around her body, hoping it would camouflage her from sight.

Satisfied, Jemima entered through the heavy, wooden front door and moved toward the phone she spied on the floor. Her eyes darting here and there she dialed, listening to the rotary motor as it returned to the proper position. Time was short and if *they* came back, she needed to have shared the message.

The phone rang once. Twice. With a brrping sound it connected.

"Hello?" A male answered and she felt a warm flush of relief at the voice. A voice she knew well.

"The manor has been breached. The girl child taken." The words erupted and her hand trembled.

"On our way." The click of the receiver being replaced echoed loudly in the stillness of the room.

Copper. She smelled copper.

Her stomach soured, knowing it meant more deaths. Jemima looked around for the gun—a gun with deadly, holy water-infused copper bullets—she knew was hidden somewhere in the room. A gun she couldn't find. *No divine intervention exists here*, she thought.

Hopefully *they* didn't remain. Feeding. If they were still here, that's what they would be doing. She found a corner and scrunched down, hiding from sight.

Crouched low, she tried to stay as still as possible, listening for sounds of the vehicles she knew would be coming. She dug her fingers into the flesh of her arms; remaining aware enough to stop before drawing blood. That would surely bring them out. Jemima dragged the cloak around her to capture the warmth, yet there was little to be found.

The sounds of engines roused her from the corner of the room. Jemima inched toward the window, the lead of the old glass distorting her view, hearing raised voices she knew Mistress Cressida had arrived.

Jemima retreated. Remained hidden from the woman because if

she knew, all may well be lost. From the shadowed room she listened to the conversation...

"It smells like Estersham." The Mistress' eyes closed. "If it is, we have a problem." She turned once more, her face set and eyes now glacial in intensity. "James?"

The man nodded as if he knew what was to come.

"If I take those steps, I cannot return. Another must stand in my place." Her voice hardened while her eyes glittered in the dim light, piercing in their intensity.

Then the Mistress' voice called out in the near silence. "You and yours have been my loyal servants for so many years. I took an oath to protect you long ago. I renewed it with marriage and births, over and over. Now, my home and yours have been breached and this child taken from us. The girl child, who will be the hope and salvation of our kind, was ripped from the bosom of our nest. I will repay your loyalty and I will get her back." The words of power rippled in the night and licked at Jemima's skin.

Available in Ebook
books2read.com/BloodBride-Nix

Direct Autographed Copy
https://www.imogenenix.net/BloodBride

ALSO BY IMOGENE NIX

<u>Warriors of the Elector</u>

- Star of Ishtar
- Starline
- Starfire
- Star of the Fleet
- Starburst
- The Star of Eternity

The Star of Ishtar & Starline - Print

Starfire & Star of the Fleet - Print

Starburst & The Star of Eternity - Print

<u>Blood Secrets</u>

- The Blood Bride
- The Illuminated Witch
- The Sorcerer's Touch

The Secrets World:

<u>Blood Secrets</u>

- The Blood Bride
- The Illuminated Witch
- The Sorcerer's Touch

<u>House Secrets</u>

- As Dawn Breaks
- Immortal Consequences
- Unnamed Book III

All That Glitters - a House Secrets Novella

Danu's Secrets

- The Downfall of Padraic O'Shaunessy
- Unnamed Secrets Book II

The Automaton Series

- Haven House
- Nobel Crest

The Search Duology

- Miss Elspeth's Desire
- Miss Isabelle's Craving

Duology World Novels

- A Very Merry Widow (coming soon)

Reunion Trilogy

- War's End
- The Assassin
- Executing Justice

The Reunion Trilogy in Paperback

Sex Love & Aliens

- Tangled Webs
- False Webs
- Covert Webs

21st Testing Protocol

- Cyborg: Redux

- Children Of A Greater Evil
- When Evil Came To Stay
- Finis: The War To End All Wars

Celtic Cupid Trilogy

- Blame The Wine
- A Stranger's Embrace
- Revenge On Cupid

The Celtic Cupid Trilogy in Paperback

Zombieology

- The Reset
- I Dream of Zombies
- The Six Million Dollar Zombie
- Make Room For Zombies
- Days of Our Zombies
- Unnamed Zobiology title (coming soon)

Knights of Pleasure

- Silken Knights

Single Titles

The Chocolate Affair (also in Print)

Falling In Love Again (Previously A Sapphire For Karina)

BioCybe (also in Print)

Hesparia's Tears (also in Print)

Tomorrow's Promise

A Bar In Paris (also in Print)

Inheritance Of The Blood (also in Print)

The Plan

Loving Memories (also in Print)

Hero of Heartbreak Hill (also in Print)

My One & Only

Curse Bound

Raspberry Dreams (Not Yet Released)

Non Fiction

Self Publishing: Absolute Beginners Guide (With Suzi Love)

Written as Ciara Cave

25 Curated Ways To Get Rid Of Telemarketers

Book Signings for Absolute Beginners

ABOUT THE AUTHOR

 Imogene is published in a range of romance genres including Paranormal, Science Fiction and Contemporary. She is mainly published in the UK and USA.

In 2010, Imogene Nix (the pen name not Imogene herself) was born. Imogene sat down and worked tirelessly for 3 months culminating in the book Starline, which became the first in a trilogy titled, "Warriors of the Elector." Since then she's had over 30 titles published and is now focusing on hybridising herself - with a mixture of traditionally published and self-published works.

In fact, she's taking control of many of her back catalogue books, which are slowly re-releasing as self-published titles.

Imogene is a member of a range of professional organisations world wide, and believes in the mantra of mentoring and paying it forward and is actively involved in mentorship (through NaNoWrimo and her vlog: In The Chair With Imogene Nix) and tutoring of new and upcoming authors.

In her spare time she loves to drink coffee, wine & eat chocolate and is parenting her spoiled dog and a ferocious cat along with her husband and daughter and looks forward to weekends away with her husband in their caravan "The Seven Year Hitch!" Do look forward to her caravan romance at some point!

To Contact Imogene
www.imogenenix.net
imogene@imogenenix.net

Sign up for her newsletter at
https://www.imogenenix.net/Signup

facebook.com/ImogeneNix
twitter.com/ImogeneNix
instagram.com/ImogeneNix
bookbub.com/authors/imogenenix